THE SCROLL
OF MAN

"The ending of the game of mankind cannot be foreseen, for the future is subject to the decisions and actions of the players. But the time will come when the condition of mankind is so reduced that even its renascences will be squalid, and it will approach the bound beyond which there can be no recovery.

"In the time of that dangerous approach will be a last chance for mankind. And shrunken though they are in power and knowledge, those who were principal players in ancient time shall gather again, in fellowship or enmity, to settle their fate and that of all mankind.

"From that forgathering will come the end of the game. And the end may be followed by a golden age. Or the game may simply grind to a stop, leaving its players mired and lost forever." —From the *Scroll of Hidden Knowledge*

"You said you'd sent a call for a warrior of special skill. I take it I'm it."

Her eyes were mysteries in the moonlight. "I called to whoever was to hear," she said. "And you were the one I called, although neither of us knew. Were you not the one, it is unlikely you would have come."

"You could have done worse."

She smiled slightly.

"What do you need with a warrior of special skills?"

"The world is in danger."

So what's new? I thought. "What kind of danger?"

"Of being destroyed."

"Destroyed? By what?"

"By God," she said.

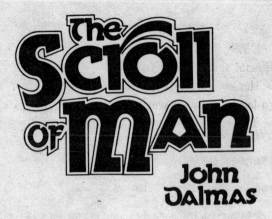

The Scroll of Man

John Dalmas

TOR

A TOM DOHERTY ASSOCIATES BOOK

To David Palter, whose knowledge of SF and of storysmithing are truly remarkable.

THE SCROLL OF MAN

Copyright © 1985 by John Dalmas

First printing: January 1985

A TOR Book

Published by Tom Doherty Associates
8-10 West 36 Street
New York, N.Y. 10018

Cover art by Ramos

ISBN: 0-812-53425-5
CAN. ED.: 0-812-53426-3

Printed in the United States of America

PROLOGUE

(From the *Scroll of Hidden Knowledge*, by
Jikan Kulo, reconstructed and translated by
Master Uno Ulao).

The beginnings of the universe and of beings are
lost in the depths of time. The earliest time known
was of beings like gods.

To make existence interesting, these entered into
games with one another, and as time went on,
formal rules were made to play by. And rewards
were added, and penalties, and restrictions on de-
parting a game. These were to add the zest of
danger and necessity to games. And beings became avid for games, and did not see, or did not
heed, where this was leading.

There were many worlds and many games. And
beings who were between games sought other
games around the universe. When the game was
created here on Ch'matal, Ch'matal was called
Weirro, which meant "game field." In time it would
have many other names, among them *Terra, Eorthe,*
and *World*. But the idea of "game field" was
forgotten.

And all who wished to play on Weirro were required to agree to limiting terms. One of the terms was that, having agreed, they would forget what the terms were, although bound by them with force. And another, they would forget the agreeing. And another, they would forget the goal of the game. And another, they would be in ignorance that it was a game. And another, they would not know who they were until such time as the game was over.

This would provide *seriousness*. It would allow *surprise*. And it required skill and application in attempting to work out what the terms, the rules of the game, were. For those who could most closely discover and play to the limits of the rules would gain the advantage. Their penalties and failures would be fewer, their successes greater.

And thus there came to be philosophy, and religion, and science.

And the purposes of the game and its rules were numerous. The most general were to experience the sensations and emotions that would grow therefrom, and to provide challenges. The goal of the game was to regain full knowledge of the agreement, which would end the game and cancel the agreement.

But the goal was hidden in forgetfulness.

And because of forgetfulness, it was decided that one named SPEKTHOS should record the game in full, with everything that happened. He was chosen because he did not care himself to play, but he preferred to watch, and had made an energy construct that stored full recordings of sight and sound and other sensings. And he was not to intervene in the game.

But the game degenerated severely, and when it was clear that those within were trapped, could not win free, SPEKTHOS determined to intervene to save them by advising those who still were perceptive enough to hear his thoughts when he addressed them. From these interventions he came to be thought of as god, or as the chief god, and many and various beliefs grew up about him in attempts to understand. And various scriptures were written, but only this one is correct.

And SPEKTHOS came to be called by many names. But since the fall of the Terrible Empire, he has most generally been called *Yough-Kalu*, "Sky Father," although by that time he himself had long since fallen and was a memory only.

Yet these interventions by SPEKTHOS only slowed the decline. By the time of Atlantis, the beings of the game were so reduced in power and intention and willingness by lifetimes of accumulating penalties, that even the greatest had lost the attributes of godliness and become what they since have been. Which is called mankind. Some were greater and some lesser, but all were mankind.

And more and more became mere pawns in the game, pressed down not only by penalties but by futility. Yet the spark of godliness persisted under the burden of not remembering and of loss, occasionally to grow to a smoldering coal.

And SPEKTHOS, afflicted by seeing the plight of his fellow beings, undertook to establish among them a continuous action whereby mankind might stay or reverse its own decline, perhaps to regain a state of knowledge and power sufficient to complete the game and release the players.

Thus, in a rude kingdom called Atlantis, he selected the highest being and established a dynasty of Guardians. And to the first Guardian he taught all the knowledge which, bound by the agreement, she yet could receive.

Then he gave her further power to help her. But because of the agreement, this power could not be pure, nor truly her own, but had to be mediated by physical means. For she was constrained by the agreement. Thus he created "the Rod of Knowing," which was a limited terminal to the game recorder, not accessing any time earlier than the origin of the rod. Also he created "the Sphere of Viewing," which would allow a Guardian to see anything accessed by the Rod of Knowing. And these he gave to the first Guardian, in trust for all Guardians to come.

Then SPEKTHOS sat back to observe and record, as originally intended and agreed. And under a series of Guardians, Atlantis flourished, becoming a great and beautiful empire of long duration, during a time when much of Ch'matal was icebound. But even that recovery collapsed under the weight of blind compulsions and penalties which resulted from the accursed accord and from the impact of natural calamity.

And SPEKTHOS then asked himself what further he might do to help mankind win free. For it seemed that the Guardians were not enough. And he decided to go among mankind garbed in a body, in human form, for in human form, all would perceive him and could be taught by him. And having not agreed to the accord, he could combine flesh with godliness of knowledge. But he did not understand the conditions of the game as fully as he thought.

And SPEKTHOS, known in the body as *Bherk-Kari*, or "Shining Person," traveled about accompanied by his students. His powers and knowledge were blunted by constant and close association with the ignorance and confusion of mankind, their fears and angers and suspicions. But still he remained in control of his purposes and intentions; he knew who and what he was, and in his wisdom he was like a god among them. And everywhere, large crowds gathered to hear his wisdom and ponder on it. Even the skeptics were drawn to him.

And his students were eight in number, and even before his coming had been wiser and more discerning than others. And he taught them privately so that they rapidly began to see and to grow in power and certainty.

And among his students, one attained the highest, and his name was *Gerthan*, but he would be known as *Shu-Gwelth*, "Accursed Liar." And Gerthan/Shu-Gwelth learned part of the trap that each man bears, and saw therewith not a means of freedom or a means to help his fellows, but a means of power and domination for himself. And he kept this hidden deep within himself, and did not look at it, for he feared he would be found out. Thus Bherk-Kari did not perceive the evil intention which was the source of the darkness about Gerthan/Shu-Gwelth.

So when they had stopped in a certain kingdom, Gerthan/Shu-Gwelth went to the king and said that Bherk-Kari planned to incite the people against him. And the king sent courtiers to Bherk-Kari to invite him to teach the king. And the courtiers went in good faith, not knowing their king intended treachery. And when Bherk-Kari came into the presence of the king, soldiers took Bherk-Kari and laid chains upon him, and he was impaled on an iron rod, and the rod was set upon the castle wall, and there Bherk-Kari died, and SPEKTHOS was thereby trapped into the cycle of lives and deaths on Ch'matal.

And he had never identified himself as *Deiwos*,

which in that time and place was the name of god. So people believed that Deiwos continued to watch over them from his place in the sky.

And Gerthan/Shu-Gwelth, with what he had learned from Bherk-Kari, became a great sorcerer, and made a kingdom for himself, and amused himself with evil. And in time retired in boredom, to sleep for a thousand years. . . .

ONE

I hit the ground so unexpectedly, I didn't even roll, and for a moment lay unmoving, feeling moist close-cropped grass against my bare legs, belly, and arms. An instant before, I'd been kicking along on touring skis through the wilderness of the Yukon Flats in a Siberian training project.

It was still night; that much was the same. Cautiously I raised my face enough to look around, and found that the night was different, too, because now the moon was up, lighting what appeared to be a garden or landscaped yard. It was the brightest moonlight I could remember. I could even, though faintly, perceive colors.

I got to my knees, kneeling upright. I expected it to be a different moon; that's how different everything felt. But it was the old familiar man-in-the-moon face that I looked at. Though maybe bigger, as if it were closer to Earth.

Someone was watching me, or some *thing* was. I cast around looking for it, spotted large golden eyes in black shadow and felt for a gun. I was as naked and unarmed as Venus, and fifteen seconds earlier I'd been in arctic uniform with a Suomi K-7 snapped to my harness.

I probed the shadow where the eyes were, trying to make out what wore them—something low to the ground, like a big dog crouching. As if to show me, it came into the light then, a large cat, leopard-like, and as best I could see, it was an indigo blue with copper-gold polygons. It sat down in a pool of moonlight and watched me.

I'd had people play cat-and-mouse with me a time or two, but never an actual cat.

I looked around. This was not a garden like my mom's. It had statues, marble benches, and shaped shrubs, with something like a palace, but much smaller—maybe a temple—looming beautifully white in the moonlight beside it. The temperature must have been about seventy-five.

[Are you ready?]

Someone had spoken the words into my mind.

It was a night for firsts. The watchcat—that's what it was, I realized, a watchcat—the watchcat had spoken to me telepathically. But maybe the most surprising thing so far was that I hadn't wondered if I'd gone nuts. I knew I was sane— sane, alert, and . . . She'd asked if I was ready.

"Ready for what?"

The watchcat stood and stretched slowly, then walked toward me, but I felt completely unthreatened. It passed about three feet away, utterly casual, four to five feet long, not counting the tail. I could have reached out and touched it. It looked at me as it went by, and I got the definite impression that I was supposed to follow. I did.

It led me toward the building, along a walk of loosely fitted white flagstones, through patches of moonlight broken by the shadows of shrubs and trees. It was a graceful building, reminiscent of some Middle Eastern architecture, but mainly it was unique.

We went to an entrance, where another watchcat, larger, lay watching us up the steps. His eyes never left me, but he was as assured and untroubled as my guide. Inside, the tall, carpeted hall was lit by moonlight; it was roofed with glass, its walls white marble. I saw no other light.

"Were you expecting me?" I asked the watchcat.

[No.]

"What am I doing here?"

[I do not know.]

That stopped me, because the whole feel of the thing was like a summons, as if I'd been called and expected and was being taken to someone who was waiting for me.

The hall led to a room, open on one side to a planted court or patio. It wasn't as light, but my eyes had adjusted, and a lot of moonlight reflected in from outside. A woman stood there, tall and slender and round, wearing something close but loose, something white down to her feet. Her hair, I knew, would be copper-colored.

White can be beautiful, no question about it. I was instantly conscious of being black and naked.

[I found him in the garden.]

"Thank you." To me she said, "Who are you?"

"Charley Judge," I said. "Sergeant First Class Charley Judge of the Twenty-Third Special Forces Unit."

"And what were you doing in my garden? Unclothed."

"Sorry about that. I have no idea. One minute I was in Alaska, wearing arctic winter uniform, and the next I was here in my birthday suit. I was hoping you could fill me in on it."

Normally a little thing like no clothes wouldn't bother me as long as it didn't bother the locals or the law. No gun I might expect to bother me, but not no clothes. But just now I wished I was dressed.

She pulled a silvery cord, then looked at me again, thoughtfully.

"You are a man of war," she said matter-of-factly.

"Right. And I speak Arabic, Russian, and Spanish, along with a little of a few others. Where did you learn English?"

"English? It is Ixma we speak."

"Hnh! All right, if you say so. Where did I learn Ixma?"

"If you need to ask, then perhaps you did not learn it. Perhaps you simply know it. Everyone else does on Ixmatl. Unlike ancient times, there is but one tongue, even on the farthest continent."

So they'd annulled Babel. But she hadn't explained anything. At best, she'd described. Or maybe this was some kind of weird dream. If it was, it had remarkable detail and internal consistency: the garden was fragrant; objects threw shadows; the carpet was soft underfoot . . . Not like any dream I could recall having. If it was a dream, it was unusually interesting.

About then a servant girl came in with a white robe and, following the woman's gesture, handed it to me and left without a word. I put it on.

"So then," the woman said, "you are a man of war. With what weapons are you skilled, Charley Judge?"

"You name it," I told her, "and chances are I'm skilled with it. Short of ballistics missiles. Rifle, heavy weapons, piano wire. I can drop a mortar round down a chimney—well, maybe not quite—and sabotage a bridge so no one will know until the trucks fall into the river. I've got black belts in four martial arts; I'm skilled with the hook sword and samurai sword, and I've been trained in ninja techniques."

Most of which was gibberish to her, but she got

the idea. "What it amounts to," I finished, "is that I'm a walking organic war machine."

She looked long at me, and I wondered what she was thinking. Then she pulled the silvery cord again. This time I felt something, felt what struck me as a thought going out, but not to me. How had the girl known to bring me a robe? Maybe the watchcat had told her. But if the watchcat could communicate telepathically, why not her mistress? There was a lot I didn't know here.

"You know something about me now," I said to her, "but you haven't even told me your name."

"I am Erolanna, the Guardian of Ixmatl."

"And Ixmatl is?"

"Ixmatl is the world. This world."

"The whole planet is Ixmatl?"

"Yes."

"And you're the ruler?"

"No. I am the guardian. There are many rulers on Ixmatl, each with his own holding. There is only one guardian."

I didn't have time to ask any more then, because this guy came in, wearing a short sword and carrying another. About my height—five-eleven—he weighed somewhat less, maybe one-eighty. And he looked bored, definitely bored.

So she was going to test me. That made sense.

"Ranzil," she said, "this is Charley Judge. I wish to see how skilled he is in arms. Give him a sword, and you two will contest." She looked at me, then back to him. "I will have neither of you badly injured."

Easier said than done, I thought. Ranzil nodded and I got rid of my robe. He scowled at me; I'm not sure whether it was because I was naked, or black, or more muscular than he was. Whatever. He wasn't scared, just hostile. I wasn't either one;

just interested. I never for a minute wondered if maybe he could take me.

Then he handed me one of the swords, and we took positions about six feet apart in the dim light.

"Ready?" said Erolanna. "Start!"

He was quick, deft, and familiar with his weapon, but his technique was dull and uninspired. Still, I was hampered by unfamiliarity with the short sword. I *love* the *daito*, the samurai sword; now there is class. And the hook sword is fun—a tricksy weapon. But the short sword is best suited to hackers. It took me the better part of twenty seconds before I kicked his feet out from under him and he crashed hard to the floor.

Erolanna called a halt and Ranzil got up. Now he *really* didn't like me. The last I saw of him that night, he was looking daggers at me as he went out the door, taking both swords with him. It occurred to me he might be her lover.

"Maybe you should have brought in someone else to test me," I said to her. "He disliked me as soon as he saw me. Now he hates my guts." I draped myself with the robe again. "I may have to end up killing him."

"He is the captain of my guard," she answered, "and my best swordsman. He provided the most meaningful test. And he will not attack you; therefore, you will not kill him."

It was interesting how she said it: It wasn't an order, just a nice simple statement of fact.

"What was going on with him?" I asked. "Is he in love with you? Or doesn't he like blacks?"

"They are very protective of the guardian. And it is tradition that the guardian be celibate. Very rarely has a guardian had a husband or lover. He worried that you might be a threat to that."

"Am I?"

She looked at me with steady eyes that would be blue by daylight but were shadowed black now, and nothing was said for several seconds.

"Among most folk," she said at last, "a woman can become as avid for a man as he for her, and as subject to poor judgment from it. But a guardian is selected from many candidates by one who sees deeply. We are innately disinclined to passion, and self-sufficient mentally and emotionally, otherwise we would not be guardian.

"Yet you are strange, different, and I find you interesting. Ranzil discerned this, and as you were naked beneath your robe, it disturbed him, although it is not his proper concern." She paused thoughtfully. "I shall have you taken to the guardsmen's quarters now, that Ranzil need feel no concern."

"Just a minute!" I said as she reached for the cord. "I've got some questions to ask, too. Do you realize what happened to me tonight? I lost my goddamned world! With zero warning I landed in your garden, either on another planet or in another time. And, lady, I'm pretty damned sure you had something to do with it, intentional or not.

"So if you want cooperation from me, how about giving me some answers? The least you could do is invite me to sit down."

None of this seemed to annoy or embarrass her in the slightest. She smiled a little, nodded, then led me down a hall and up a flight of stairs to a large balcony, where we sat down on a cushioned marble bench. For a while we talked, then, more or less to my surprise, moved on to other things. Her lips were soft and cool, her eyes open and enigmatic. And she was in control, not of me but of herself. She was different than any other woman

I'd known, a new experience I'd have to digest before I could evaluate.

I felt a little worried about it afterward, although she didn't seem to. On a personal level, if she decided it was a good time to stop being a virgin, that was her decision and my good fortune. But, on the other hand, she had a position here, a part she was supposed to play. For this whole planet, apparently. And I didn't want anything bad to come of our little romp. But she seemed cool about it—even serene. After a bit I broke the silence.

"You said you'd sent a call for a warrior of special skill. I take it I'm it. How did you do that?"

Her eyes were mysteries in the moonlight. "I called to whoever was to hear," she said. "You heard."

"I don't remember hearing anything—anyone calling me, that is. I was skiing across a muskeg with seven other guys, and some solitary old he-wolf howled up along the ridge. Then I looked up at the northern lights, thinking how appropriate they were with a wolf howl, and zap! Here I was."

She nodded. "I did not call with the voice. That would have been futile. And you were the one I called, although neither of us knew. Were you not the one, it is unlikely you would have come."

"You could have done worse."

She smiled slightly.

"What do you need with a warrior of special skills?"

"The world is in danger."

So what's new? I thought. "What kind of danger?"

"Of being destroyed."

"Destroyed? By what?"

"By God," she said.

TWO

It was as pretty a day as you could ask for, the sky mostly soft blue, with occasional stacked white clouds aspiring to be thunderheads. I wore roman boots, bleached linen kilt, a sleeveless open shirt, and short sword.

I'd sketched a samurai sword for Bressir, the armor artificer—all its details and the steps in its proper construction—and given him the dimensions I wanted. When he delivered an acceptable product, maybe he could graduate to a pistol.

The watchcat and I climbed a broad rounded ridge through thin grass speckled finely with small white flowers. Below us, to the east, lay rolling vineyards and fields bordered with low heaped walls of loose stone, and occasional broad-crowned pines. Beyond them, some miles off, were low mountains dark with forest.

To the west we looked down on grassland like that we were hiking through, undulating to the rim of cliffs a mile away. Beyond that, the ocean, or maybe just a sea; the geography still was a mystery to me.

Other things were, too, although our talk the night before had helped. But a little mystery doesn't bother me; it keeps things interesting. And I've never been strongly attached to any place; the past doesn't hold me, and I'm light on my feet about the future.

So Ixmatl was fine with me. So far.

We'd talked until the nearly full moon was well into the west. God, she said, had told her he was tired of the world and its people. Things hadn't turned out at all like he'd had in mind, and he was getting ready to trash the planet. Unless she could straighten it out. No, she'd said, he hadn't appeared in a vision or otherwise. And no, there hadn't been any voice. Just his thoughts entering her mind.

What had happened to me—my arrival, the bigger, brighter moon, a telepathic leopard/watch-cat—might make a lot of strange reports believable, but somehow I couldn't buy the idea that there was a god named Juokal getting ready to blow the place up.

Where I fitted in was, I was to be her leg man. And when it was over, I might even be able to go back home if I wanted to. To 1987, that is. I hadn't really thought of any *place* as home since I'd got out of high school in St. Clair Shores, Michigan. I'd already decided on a career then, and while I'd graduated with honors, my central interest was the martial arts, complete with their philosophy, with strong minors in gymnastics and hockey. And books, all kinds of books. I thrived on five hours of sleep a night, even then.

She claimed to have a time machine, and after what had happened, I could accept that more easily than I could Juokal. But she insisted she hadn't transferred me here with it—that my arrival out of the past had been totally unexpected and on my own. Regardless of how it might have felt to me. As she described it, it wasn't a regular machine, with bus bars and circuit boards. It was more like magic, but apparently followed regular laws of some kind. The science of magic.

Supposedly, Juokal had intended that man would gradually overcome his obstacles and build a grander and grander civilization on Earth. But, instead, we'd gone through cycles of development and collapse. And after a while, each consecutive climb had been to a lesser height than the one before. Just now they were supposed to be in sort of a high, but it was a world of nobles and peasants, warlords and barbarism. The district I was looking at now was supposed to be one of the best of the lot, being closest to the Guardian of Ixmatl.

Well, if Juokal was the creator, I'd say the responsibility was his. If he'd screwed the job up, he shouldn't be all that upset if mankind couldn't make it go right.

Me, I've never felt like anyone's creation. I'm just me. And I've never felt like passing the buck to any god or like I had to live up to his expectations.

"Watchcat," I said, "what's your name? I feel like, if we're going to be around each other much, I ought to call you something besides Watchcat."

[Watchcat is name enough.]

"Okay, Watchcat it is. Are all cats on Ixmatl intelligent like you?"

[Only the guardian's watchcats. There are three of us, and we are more than cats. We are like you.]

"Explain."

I picked up a sense of patience, as with a decent adult explaining to a child.

[We are . . . beings like you. But born with cat bodies. And we do not have or need names: We know who is addressing, or being called or referred to. If it is useful to you, however, you may give me a name.]

"Hmm. What name would you like?"

I got a sense of shrugging.

"How about Diana, then? Diana was the goddess of the hunt, a long time ago, and leopards are traditionally great hunters. Or were in my time. She's also the goddess of the moon, and I saw you first by moonlight."

There was no response, as if the whole thing was too trivial to talk about further. A piercing whistle sounded far overhead, and I paused to watch a circling hawk. Or it might have been a kite, for the tail was deeply forked, although the wings were somewhat broad and not pointed. It might have been an example of evolution since my time.

[Charley Judge,] the watchcat thought to me, [I did not intend aloofness by my delay in answering. You are a strange person, and I was evaluating, considering you. I will be honored to be known by you as Diana.]

"Why, thanks, Diana. That's a hell of a nice compliment. I wasn't sure you'd like me this morning."

There was a sense of questioning.

"You know what happened last night, don't you? Between Erolanna and me?"

[Of course.]

"I thought you might disapprove. Do you?"

[I will disapprove of any ill effects. If she fully retains her powers and judgment, the integrity and rationality of her actions, there will be nothing of which to disapprove. I will not criticize in advance.]

Fair enough, I thought.

We had reached the broad undulant crest of the ridge we'd been climbing. And now, about two hundred yards ahead, a group of horsemen appeared over a rise. There were five of them. Two carried birds on their arms, one of them an eagle. They saw us and pulled up. For an interval we watched each other; then the man with the eagle removed its hood and released it.

The bird rose sharply with strong wing beats, and I was surprised by a sense of anger from the watchcat. With no hesitation the eagle flew toward us; Watchcat crouched down, snarling, as it hurtled. It darted at the leopard, then tilted away at the last instant to avoid a lightning paw.

It ignored me, and I drew my short sword as it wheeled around to swoop again. In mid-swoop it swerved, screaming, and darted toward me. Again it changed direction at the last moment as my sword flicked out. Instead of halving the bird, as I'd had in mind, only the tips of some flight feathers drifted to the ground.

But that was enough for the eagle. Screaming again, it beat upward a few wild strokes, then sped for its master.

"What in the hell was that all about?" I asked, my eyes following its flight.

[It is more than bird, as I am more than cat,] she said, and there was anger with the thought. [Its master is Lord Cratlik, who rules this district. He is a magician of sorts—the bird is his familiar.]

It landed again on his forearm. Now he sent one of his companions jogging his horse toward us, and I started off at a lope to meet him. When Cratlik saw this, he halted his man and they waited. As I got closer, I could see Cratlik was smiling. It wasn't particularly ugly or threatening, but no way was it friendly. I got the idea of someone who enjoyed something happening, something different and interesting going on, and didn't care a whole hell of a lot what it was. A man who could kill someone just for the hell of it.

The stooge who'd started for me was something else; his expression was sheer and total hatred, and we'd never even seen each other before. He sat his horse almost in line between me and Cratlik; I decided to take him without warning. As I approached, he drew his sword, and I slowed to a brisk walk, empty-handed, then made as if to pass him as he nudged his horse into my way.

I twitched my knife from its sheath. He screamed, clutching at the front of his shoulder, his sword falling to the ground, and I leaped, jerking him from the saddle. He screamed again as he hit; with a seven-inch blade in his deltoid, I didn't blame him.

His was a war-horse; it didn't break. I grabbed the reins while glancing at Cratlik. He looked surprised but not upset. I mounted to the saddle. His other three retainers looked ready to carve me up, but their master decided to be amused.

"Cratlik," I said, gesturing at the man on the ground, "what do you keep an ugly moron like that around for?"

His smile disappeared. "You use my familiar name to me," he charged.

I chose to misunderstand. "The watchcat told me who you are. She and the guardian. I resent your siccing that half-assed chicken on her."

Apparently Cratlik decided that that much arrogance just might have something formidable behind it; he elected a look-first approach to me. He examined the bird thoughtfully, the fingers of his bare hand stroking it, then gently extended the right wing. The now-hooded bird hissed. Letting the wing close against its side again, Cratlik turned his eyes to me. His lips pursed thoughtfully.

"I do not know you," he said.

"My name is Charley Judge; I serve the Guardian of Ixmatl as her chief aid." I hoped she wouldn't mind the self-appointment. "I'm a good man to have as a friend, and I'm easy to get along with. But horseshit like that annoys me." I gestured at the man sitting on the ground with tears of pain and rage on his gray face. He'd pulled the knife out and was staring at it.

"You!" I snapped at him. "On your feet!"

He looked up, hating me more than before. "I'm hurt," he husked.

"You don't know what hurt is yet," I said, and reined the horse around while digging my right heel into its flank. The hard hooves thudded close, and with a little cry, the man scrambled out of the way on hands and knees.

"Up!" I ordered, "and hand me my knife, hilt first. Now!"

He did. His sleeve and the left side of his shirt were soggy with blood, and the knife blade was smeared with it.

"Wipe it first, fool," I snarled. He wiped it on his kilt, then reached it toward me again. I took it and returned it to its sheath.

"Thank you," I said in a reasonable voice. "What is your name?"

"Lurz," he said thickly.

"Lurz," I said, "you have met Charley Judge. You did not fare badly, compared to others who've threatened me. I allowed you to live because you didn't know me." Then I moved the horse at him, backing him away from the vicinity of his fallen sword. He was psychotic, and he'd gladly have died right then and there, if he thought he could take me with him. I'd probably have to kill him sooner or later, unless someone else did it for me.

But this wasn't the time. I'd already stretched my luck and Cratlik's tolerance.

I turned to him and grinned. So far I'd given an Oscar performance; actually I am not a mean mother. "Why *did* you do that?" I asked, "sic the eagle on the watchcat? You knew who she belongs to."

His eyes were not friendly, but they weren't hostile yet either. "For amusement," he said. "It pleased me to. And it would not have injured the beast." He looked down at his bird and stroked it, then back up at me, challengingly. "Had you killed my Glinda, my men would be skinning you right now."

He was testing me, a test it would be well to pass. "Ah well," I said, "it all worked out. Being skinned is for lesser men, not for the likes of me or you. That's why our actions are never so far from correct as to bring on such misfortunes." I laughed. "We each have a guiding spirit looking out for us. I happen to be my own. Who is yours?"

The idea pleased him and fitted his reality; he laughed with me. "And I am mine," he said. "I've never found another I could trust that far. In judgment, that is." He gestured at his three mounted men. "These stout fellows are valued for their loyalty and skill at arms, but as for wits, I rely upon my own alone."

I nodded. "Loyal men with good weapons skills are always to be valued, as long as they are not a liability to their lord. But those of exceptional intelligence and force of spirit are more valuable than jewels.

"This is a fine horse," I added, changing the subject. "Let me ride him home. I'll send him back to you tomorrow."

"No," said Cratlik. "You may ride him, but you may not return him. It would offend me. He is a gift to you—his name is Groll—a token of my friendship to the Guardian of Ixmatl and to a most remarkable man."

I bowed slightly in the saddle. "You are generous, and an aristocrat in the fullest sense. My thanks and good wishes go with you."

I turned and kicked the horse into an easy trot, the watchcat following me from where she had stopped some hundred yards from my encounter. I hoped my indifferent horsemanship wasn't conspicuous. When I looked back, some distance on, it was to see the horsemen moving over the rise and out of sight. Nobody had picked up Lurz; he was stumbling along on foot, holding his shoulder.

I wondered if he'd make it home, or if he'd bleed to death while I rode his horse.

THREE

By the end of the day, Ranzil had decided I was okay after all. He was a genuine company man, wanted Erolanna to have the best household troops possible, and was beginning to see me as an ally. I'd given them a demonstration of unarmed techniques, broke a few boards (which they loved), and showed them some sword techniques. Afterward I told him I'd be happy to help train them, if he'd like, and he took me up on it.

The troops thought it was a great idea, too, when he told them, and I started the same day training the off-duty watches. You could feel the change in attitude at once; there's nothing like the prospect of improvement and accomplishment to bring someone from boredom to enthusiasm. Now I'd have to make time to deliver, but I could do that. And once they'd made a little progress, they'd be able to work on it without me when I couldn't be there.

I also made a point of eating with the troops. After supper a household servant came and took me to Erolanna's study. Or office. Or maybe lab.

"So you have a horse," she said.

She was so damned lovely, it was hard to believe. And powerful. And sure of herself.

"I intended to tell you when I saw you," I answered. "How'd you find out?"

"I questioned the watchcat. Incidentally, she regards you very highly. Then I viewed the whole affair in—here, let me show you."

She walked to a stand, and on it there was— honest to god!—a crystal ball! A clear crystal sphere about fifteen inches in diameter, not very heavy.

"How does it work?" I asked.

"I see things in it," she said. "I can see any place and past time I wish." It took light and life in her hands, and suddenly I was watching Watchcat and me standing on the grassy ridge with the eagle flying toward us. In three dimensions. I watched it attack, and myself drawing my sword; then she turned it off and put it back on the stand.

"Hey," I said, "now *that* is something! This operation is starting to look better and better.

"Do you approve of the way I handled things out there?"

She smiled. "Under very treacherous circumstances you obtained a surprisingly good result. Cratlik is not truly your friend, despite the gift, but he is not your enemy. You have his respect and his curiosity.

"Lurz, of course, will kill you if he can, but he might well have killed or maimed you there before you could even have identified yourself.

"Yes, you did well indeed."

It was getting dark. She walked over to a faceted crystal about the size of a grapefruit, gestured, and it took on a white glow. I stared; no wires. "Boss," I told her, "working for you is going to be interesting and educational."

She laughed, a nice light laugh. "We shall see what you think of your first job. I want you to kidnap a man from your own time."

Her strategy was to have me kidnap key historical figures—people she felt had caused history to
take a wrong course—and lock them up on Ixmatl
before they'd had a chance to screw up the past.
The idea was to change history for the better. I
had no idea whether such a thing could work, but
starting with someone from my own time seemed
a good way to begin. I'd be familiar with the situation there. "Who?" I asked.

"Professor Wilhelm Wundt."

"Who?"

"Professor Wilhelm Wundt. Have you never heard
of him? He was a professor of psychology at the
University of Leipzig, in a nation called Germany.
He was born in 1832, by your system of reckoning,
and died in 1920. You will pick him up in 1856,
before he has a chance to have any meaningful
impact on history."

My face must have fallen a foot. My own time! I
suddenly realized—really realized—what I was up
against. This Wundt might be the only one she
wanted kidnaped who was within centuries of my
time. So there I'd be, a black American in nineteenth century Germany, where probably not one
person in five hundred spoke English. I knew very
little about the Germany of 1856, and remembered
maybe forty words from high school German. And
I was supposed to kidnap someone there.

"What is the matter, Charley Judge?" she asked.

I verbalized it for her; telepaths have their
limitations.

"It will be easier than you think," she said. "Let
me show you."

She went to a table and picked up another crystal,
this one a several-sided rod, about a foot long,
with pointed ends.

"I use this to learn what events, what movements,

what persons past guardians have adjudicated were important, and in what regards. From this I decide what time and place or person I wish to observe."

That seemed to imply that there had been guardians at least as far back as the nineteenth century. "When was the first guardian?" I asked.

"It was in a kingdom called Atlantis." She didn't stop to let me ask more questions. "Now, when I know when and whom or where I wish to view, I use the viewing sphere. The time machine, in turn, I control with the sphere. It is really very simple. Are you ready?"

"You mean—right now?"

"Of course."

"Well, uh, don't you think we should make some plans? Familiarize me with the person's surroundings—things like that? Get me some clothes from that period? Maybe learn some German?"

She laughed a light musical laugh. I didn't think it was funny at all. "That won't be necessary. Truly, Charley Judge, this really is much simpler than you imagine. Look."

She picked up the viewing sphere and held it between us. A three-dimensional image of a young man appeared, reading a book in a somewhat disorderly room.

"That is he: Wilhelm Wundt, in 1856 a student at the University of Berlin. He is alone in his room. See? I will put you right behind him. You need only grasp him with your hands or arms and I'll return you together at once."

She was right; that *was* simple. About as simple as it could be.

"Why do *I* need to be there?" I asked. "Why not just scoop him up without me?"

"It is a matter of intention. His transit will originate at that end, and I need your intention there in order for him to cross."

"One other thing," I said. "When I arrived here in your garden, I was naked and unarmed. Am I going to arrive there the same way?"

"No. You arrived here without benefit of the time diagram. With the diagram, everything in the rhombus is transported."

"Have you tested this?"

"Of course," she said patiently.

"Um." For the life of me I couldn't think of a damned other thing that might conceivably be a problem. Except, of course, that the time machine would have to work. *What the hell*, I thought. "Okay, let's do it."

That turned on her smile again, and we went to the complex geometric design on the floor. There she showed me where to stand—in a diamond-shaped sort of figure about six feet across. Painted lines connected it to other shapes with different things in them—some looking like abstract sculptures of copper, gold, and silver wires, but mostly crystals of one shape or another. She was great for crystals. I told myself that this might be as logical and functional as a twentieth century aircraft design, but beneath it all I couldn't imagine it would actually do anything.

When she had me positioned, she held up the crystal sphere and looked into it. From where I stood, I could see a picture appear in it. She looked over at me reassuringly, then back to the sphere. For just a brief instant I felt sort of suspended.

And *whap*! There I was. But not in Wundt's room! I was standing on a brick-paved street in a city at night, having materialized so close in front of this old guy that he walked into me before he could stop.

"Was ist los!" he said angrily.

"Oh shit!" I answered. I might not be naked, but a kilt, roman boots, and short sword were hardly street wear in Berlin in 1856.

"God damn it, Erolanna, bring me back!" I yelled, but nothing happened.

The old guy was pretty upset to have this weird-looking African materialize right in his face and then yell like that in some foreign language. He gripped his stout walking stick more like a saber than a club and backed away a couple of steps. Other people had seen, too, or at least heard me holler, and some were coming over.

And I was afraid to move. I didn't know whether she'd lose me or not if I moved, or if she could find me if she lost me. *"God damn it, Erolanna, get me back there NOW!"*

And still nothing happened. The old guy was scowling at me, his brows gnarled up over his eyes like hairy fists. He had a scar across his left jaw and cheek, and a snuff-stained white mustache that jutted upward at the ends like a boar's tusks. I didn't feel good about him at all.

Then, quick as a snake, he thrust the end of the walking stick at my face. I barely parried it with the side of my hand, and as quickly he snapped it around like a saber; the old son-of-a-bitch was military! I blocked that one with a forearm, which hurt, and kicked his feet out from under him. Then a big husky guy charged into me, clutching, and this well-dressed dude started beating on me with his cane while someone began yelling *"Polizei! Polizei!"* I knew what that meant without looking it up. I dropped the big guy, swept the beau brummel into the gutter with a spin kick, and jumped back to the approximate location I'd arrived on.

The old guy was getting laboriously up, his cane still in his fist. He didn't come at me, though—he'd seen me work, and he was a pro, not a fool. A policeman was running toward me, dressed like an old-timey soldier, with no apparent gun, but a saber in his hand. The several onlookers were keeping well back now.

I gave Erolanna about three more seconds, then turned and took off.

People got out of my way. The street wasn't crowded—it was a fairly narrow, minor-seeming street, and night—but I got a lot of attention in my bleached linen kilt and stripped to the waist. The police whistle kept blowing but got farther away.

Slowing to a trot, I turned into a sidestreet, an alley fronted by old brick structures. By "old," I mean they already looked old in 1856. They were narrow row buildings, mostly three stories tall, and I'd guess most of them were flats. Most showed soft yellowish light in one or more windows—gaslights, I suppose—but others were dark.

It was time to get some clothes; I'd be a lot less conspicuous.

I didn't see anyone at all. There was a gas street lamp about every two hundred feet, and a little light escaped through windows, but with an overcast night sky and buildings crowding close on both sides, it was darker than any city street I'd known.

I slowed to a walk. Ahead was a four-story building about thirty feet wide that looked like a stack of rental rooms, so I turned in there, bounding up the several steps and through the door.

The entryway was weakly lit by a single gaslight. A narrow hall led to the back of the building, with doors on both sides, bypassed by narrower stairs that climbed darkly to the upper stories. If there was trouble, I preferred it at street level, so I walked softly to the end of the hall instead of trying the staircase. At the last door on my right, I stopped and rapped quietly; there was no answer. I rapped again, a little louder; still nothing. I tried the knob; locked.

I didn't have anything to pick the lock with, and my shortsword was too thick to force the bolt. Maybe, I thought, I ought to go back out and mug someone in the street for clothes. Instead, I rapped on the door opposite.

"Wer ist da?"

It was a man's voice, and fortunately my high school German covered that much.

"Karl," I answered, muffling my voice with my hand. He must surely have a friend named Karl.

The voice inside said something I missed; there were too many words. But the sounds of movement I understood well enough. Someone was moving around, more than necessary, then coming to the door. I waited, light on my feet. Someone was also coming down the stairs to my left. A key rattled in the lock; the knob turned; the door opened a foot or so, and a face peered out.

It was Wundt!

He saw it was a stranger and tried to close the door, but I threw my weight against it, driving him back. He was not a trusting soul; he had a stove poker in his hand. It was probably a good thing; otherwise, he might have yelled. As it was, he tried to take care of me himself, as I shut the door behind me with a foot. A knife hand to the Adam's apple closed his act.

I took time to lock the door. "Erolanna," I muttered, "you pulled it off." Or had she? Had she led me here somehow, or had I done it myself in some unknowing way? With that last thought, a wave of chills ran over me. I crouched beside Wundt and took hold of his wrist, feeling for the pulse. It was strong and regular.

Lady, I thought, *get on the stick and pick us up.* Four seconds later she did.

FOUR

I laid the unconscious body on a pallet in a room off her lab and we waited there for more than half an hour, Erolanna and I. At first we waited for him to wake up. But then, after three or four minutes, I checked his pulse again and it had gotten unexpectedly weak. It became progressively weaker, and his breathing almost imperceptible.

"You hit him too hard," she said to me. I didn't answer. After a bit he died. She didn't say anything more, but her lips were tight with anger.

"Where do you want him?" I asked.

She shrugged, not with indifference but hostility. *Come off it, white-assed broad,* I thought. *I gave him a careful knife hand to the throat. Didn't crush his larynx or a damn thing. And his pulse was strong, seconds before you pulled us in. Then here, all of a sudden, he was fading.*

Your thoughts aren't private around Erolanna.

"Then why?" she challenged.

"Maybe bringing him across," I said. "Maybe he couldn't take it."

"You took it," she answered. "You traveled in both directions. Without harm. What happened to

37

Wilhelm Wundt is that you hit him too hard and killed him."

"Go to hell," I said, and walked out. I strode down the long hall to the main entrance, passing the big male watchcat without giving him a word or thought. The moon had just risen, a trifle flattened tonight. Twenty-four hours earlier, I thought, or maybe twenty-four thousand years earlier, I'd been skiing in the Alaskan wilderness.

How far into the future *had* I come? Hell, for all I knew, it could have been a hundred thousand years. A million. Was a day still twenty-four hours? Something had happened to make the moon move closer; maybe the day length was different, too.

Damn it! I had not killed Wundt! I thought angrily. Matter of fact, I'd never killed anyone. I'd trained and trained in deadly arts, but never had killed anyone. Could I? If I had to?

Hell, yes, I told myself. I could kill Lurz and never turn a hair. And for all I knew, Wundt was twice as bad. At least Erolanna considered him a serious factor in the degeneration of mankind.

But I had not killed him. I had a fine, highly tuned touch. I could use a knife hand to break an inch-thick board or thrust it out like a flash and touch a water glass without knocking it over. And I hadn't been out of control. I'd gotten fairly deeply into the philosophy and mental drills that, in the orient, are, were, associated with the martial arts. I can get pissed or enthused, but I don't go out of control. It was a quality that had put me in charge of several missions, back in my time.

I hadn't killed Wundt, but I didn't know what had.

Something moved in the shadows, and my eyes went to it. Watchcat was coming toward me from near the garden wall.

"Hi, Diana," I said to her, "what's happening?"

[Very little. You are troubled.]

Right. D'you know what it's about? What's going on?"

[I know what's happening with you, Charley Judge. You are stuck to an unpleasant mystery, and it has exasperated you.]

I stared at her, then laughed. "Diana, you are the *damnedest* cat! You got it exactly! Do you also know that Erolanna's mad at me?"

The watchcat nodded mentally. [*Was* mad at you. Her attention is on other things now.]

"Such as?"

[I don't know. I seldom pry. I notice the obvious, the readily apparent, but unless there is reason, I do not delve more deeply into her thoughts. Or yours.]

I really looked at her now. "Watchcat—Diana"— I said, "you are something very special. One of my favorite people of all time. Maybe number one. I not only like you, I admire hell out of you."

It was Erolanna's thought that came to me next, and I turned to see her walking from the entry into the moonlight toward us. [You are very discerning,] she thought to me. [Watchcat *is* an exceptional being. Her wisdom is simple and direct. She is the only being I ever counsel with, or was, until you came.]

She went from thought to speech as she approached. "I regret my asperity of a few minutes ago. It was inexcusable. I was disturbed and found the wrong reason for it. Finding, and accepting, wrong reasons is a principal weakness of humans. Without it, Juokal would be greatly pleased with us, I am convinced." She extended a hand to me as she reached us. "My apologies, Charley Judge."

I stood there dumb. What a fantastic woman! Here I was in a world that threatened to kill me young, in the midstride of my prime, and I considered myself lucky.

"Did you find the right reason," I asked, "for feeling disturbed?"

"Yes." She turned her attention to Watchcat. "Have you noticed any change in the world during the last hour?"

Diana examined the question. [No. But I'm not sure that we would. It might be as if the replaced conditions had never existed.]

"We would notice failure," said Erolanna. "If we had removed Wundt, it would be as if he'd never existed. We would have no further attention on him. And yet we do." She turned to me. "You took Wundt from his own time while he was still a student, before he did any of the things he would have done. I anticipated some basic changes in Ixmatl—conceivably including our own nonexistence—and surely these would be accompanied by the forgetting of Wundt."

"Mistaken identity, then," I offered. "We got the wrong man."

She shook her head. "That is not possible. By the nature of the means."

"Then maybe there is such a thing as predestination. Maybe the principal features of any time are so fixed that if someone is removed from the past, other things fill in and compensate for the removal."

She looked thoughtful. "It is very unlikely. It is at variance with our basic understandings. If our basic principles were erroneous, I would not expect our technology to be as successful as it is. And it accomplishes some remarkable things: I just sent you 3,147,805 years into the past—and brought you back."

That long! I stood there with my mouth hanging open. *That long*! I knew this datum was going to generate a lot of questions in my mind over the next few days, but just then I was struck dumb. I shook myself out of it.

"Speaking of bringing me back," I said, "you had me worried for a while. What went wrong? How'd I come out on the street instead of in Wundt's apartment?"

"I do not know. I sent you through with the viewing sphere showing Wundt's room, and you did not appear there as expected. It was quite a shock; I had no idea where you might be, or when. I kept the sphere on Wundt's room, hoping, letting it run forward in time at a normal rate; at the moment I couldn't think of anything else to do." She smiled slightly. "I have a theory, though. I believe there was a human factor operating that threw things off."

"Such as?"

"Such as you, Charley Judge. I believe you are a person in sudden growth, exploring your power. Perhaps despite yourself. As an explanation, it is consistent with the principle of the time diagram. And that was, you know, quite a demonstration, arriving in Wundt's room on your own as you did."

"On my own." There it was again, and there went the chills again, waves of them running over me, Erolanna's eyes on me seeing god knows what. After that I became aware that we were alone; Watchcat had left. We walked back to the palace together.

"So what do we do next?" I asked. "Picking up Wundt made no difference. Was he a wrong target, not so important to history as you'd thought? Will it make any difference to pick up someone else?"

She took my hand as we went in. "We will have to find out," she murmured close to my ear. "But not now. Not tonight."

FIVE

I was up early the next morning, worked out a bit, soaked briefly in a hot bath, dumped a bucket of cold water over myself, dressed, ate breakfast, and finished exploring the palace.

I spent the rest of the morning working with the troops—some with each off-duty watch. There was only one I really didn't like. He was a joker of the wrong kind. You know the type. His humor invariably put someone down. Degraded them, made them feel self-conscious. The tough he joked about when they weren't there, and only subtly. The more vulnerable he needled in their presence. When one complained, his response was, "What's the matter? Can't you take a joke?"

Some things really don't change. So about the end of the session I really jumped on him about it, verbally, really blasted him. When I was done, everyone there had a different viewpoint of him.

Lunches were pretty standard: coarse bread with butter, cheese, fruit of some kind—that day it was cherries—and warm milk from the morning milking that hadn't had time to sour yet.

After that I went to Erolanna's study.

"Hello, Charley Judge," she said, "I expected

42

you. Last night you told yourself you would have
many questions to ask."

"Yeah. Last night you said you'd sent me back
three million years to 1856. How long have there
been guardians?"

"If I recall correctly, the first guardian was appointed 3,179,014 years ago. In Atlantis."

Atlantis! My god! "And there's only one guardian
at a time?"

"That is right."

"And it's been like that for more than three
million years?"

She nodded.

"And nothing has ever broken the string? Not
once?"

"Never. There have been periods, some of them
long, when the guardians hid themselves from
the knowledge of man, concealed in anonymity
or secluded places. But continuity has been re-
tained."

Man, that threw me into a quandary. Because I
couldn't believe it. I mean, that's like a hundred
thousand generations, or a hundred and fifty
thousand! It was incredible to me that in all that
time nothing had happened to screw it up. Everything else had been.

I looked at her carefully. "So what would happen if an earthquake swallowed this place tomorrow and you were never seen again? Would that
be the end of the guardians?"

She smiled. "Not at all. There are three alive
who have been guardians before me. And disasters
shun guardians and those who have been guardians.
And each who has been a guardian after her retire-
ment trains a candidate for guardian. Indeed, each
emeritus guardian at all times has a candidate in
training. In five years another will take my place—

sooner, if I wish it or am unable to continue. But guardians seldom lay aside their office early, whether by volition or disability or death. Occasionally a guardian's powers will wane, usually from some misdeed she has done, and she will remove herself, or be removed by those who have served before. A guardian retired remains interested and aware."

"Okay. And who decides which candidate will be the new guardian?"

"The guardian herself, with the concurrence of those who served before."

It sounded okay. But it still amazed me that the system—*any* human system—had come through three million years.

"How long have you been guardian?" I asked.

"Thirty-five years."

"Thirty-five years!! You?"

She smiled, and two of the most beautiful dimples formed little commas near the corners of her mouth. "Since I was twenty," she added.

That somehow shook me more than falling three million years into her garden. Fifty-five years old and her dimples were still dimples! And a fantastic body! She could easily pass for twenty-five. A term recurred to me—the science of magic. It sure as hell wasn't just diet and exercise.

"What does a guardian do?" I asked.

"We influence events."

"What do you mean, 'influence events?' "

"With the rod of knowledge we monitor events. We watch for certain indicators. From them we locate and observe what appear to be the most critical situations, good or bad, in human affairs. Then we influence the thoughts of key persons in the direction of human betterment, as our wisdom indicates."

"How good is your wisdom? Where does it come from?"

I wasn't challenging her. It was a question I needed to ask, if I was to get any useful sort of understanding. She made the distinction. "The rod of knowledge records all that happens on Ixmatl," she answered, "from the affairs of kings and wizards to the comings and goings of meadow mice. From it we can learn whatever we wish of what has happened, using it to guide the viewing sphere. But only what has *happened*; it says nothing of thoughts or intentions.

"Still, so much is available that it would be useless without evaluation; part of our training helps us ask for the important information. To aid me in this, I spend hours each day requesting summaries from the rod and viewing the highlights."

"Summaries?" I tried to imagine some kind of printout.

"In the form of thought."

My god! A kind of universal data bank! It stunned me. More information than anyone in my time had imagined, I thought. It was wisdom that was short, as it had always been, the understanding that could adequately *use* the data.

Then it occurred to me that, with the rod and the sphere, she could resurrect science and technology! I wondered if maybe they had, in the past, and didn't want to anymore. If the tappable petroleum was gone, or the accessible high grade ores. Or maybe they'd come up with nuclear weapons a time or two too often.

"Where did you get these things—the rod and the sphere?" I asked.

"They were given to the first guardian by Juokal, although he wasn't called Juokal at that time."

Juokal again. An interventionist god was no more

unbelievable than a lot of things here, but it still felt phony to me. I didn't know why, offhand, but it did.

"And you influence the thoughts of key people. Does that mean you sneak ideas into their minds? Cause them to do things they wouldn't do otherwise?"

"In a way. There is no coercion; that is not possible. But we introduce ideas, questions, information into their thoughts, and they think of them as their own. They make of them what they will."

"Okay, then," I said bluntly, "with power like that and tools like the rod and the sphere, how come things have gone so poorly for more than three million years?"

That was a hard shot, though not a cheap one; some of the light and beauty went out of her face. But I saw no resentment; just a flinch.

"I can only say that we successfully avert many misfortunes, and even catastrophes," she answered. "We can observe that things would be much worse without us. But that is not always consolation when we look at the march of history.

"We have three principal limitations," she went on. "One is information unknown at the time of need. Harmful things will happen and often recur or continue for years and years before their effects call our attention to them. A second is the limited number of people we can work with. While the large majority of people are susceptible to our influence, we can work with relatively few, for we can touch only one at a time. Our effect on mankind must come from selecting well.

"But there is a third limitation which may be the most severe. For there are some people, some of the most harmful, whom we cannot influence at all. They persist unaffected in their destructive acts, as if they were in the grip of some evil force. In positions of power or influence, such people do great harm. We call them *ruiners*."

"Wait a minute," I said. "Are you telling me that if there's someone you can't influence with your powers, that person is bad?"

"No, Charley Judge, that is not what I meant to communicate to you." She looked sober as all hell now. "There are others whom we can influence little, or at least infrequently. The strength of their own evaluations, purposes, and decision—indeed, their own wisdom—is overriding. It is as if they have little need of outside thoughts or even information. Somehow they will manage to do the best thing. We *learn* from them. Unfortunately they are rare.

"Those I referred to before, the ruiners, are quite different. When we locate them, it is by the harm they do. We can assist those who oppose them, and to some extent counter their effects on those they operate through, but we are unable to touch them mentally.

"Occasionally a guardian has arranged the murder of such a one—in extreme cases. But this is likely to be of only limited use. For often these people operate behind the scenes and may have done great harm through others before we discover them as the source. By then much of the damage is done.

"While guardians who have turned to assassination have almost always declined in power and rationality, often very quickly."

I interrupted. "These baddies you can't influence—these ruiners—you said it was as if they were in the grip of some evil force. What do you think that evil force might be?"

"I do not know that there is one. It is only *as if*

there was one. It was a simile used in the absence of knowing." She brightened then. "Ah! You are thinking of a devil, the prince of evil, as in some ancient religions. But there is no devil, only devilish persons."

"Look," I said, "I wasn't thinking about somebody with horns and a pitchfork. But if you've got a Juokal there, which I don't believe, why not somebody with more or less comparable power, lying back out of sight, or camouflaged, like some of the human baddies you talked about? Or maybe somebody who's like the opposite of a guardian?"

She didn't answer right away. When she spoke again, it was thoughtfully. "Juokal did not mention such a one in the wisdom he gave to the first guardian. If there is one, he has come among us since then. But Juokal has rarely spoken to a guardian after the first."

Her mood changed then, and she looked at me directly. "The most promising approach I know of is to remove certain critically destructive individuals from history."

"Why hasn't anyone tried that before?" I asked.

"Until now, no one had the means of reaching back in time. We could look back, but not touch what we saw. I originated the time diagram only recently."

It occurred to me that I was sitting there hassling a genius. "It didn't work with Wundt," I pointed out. "There's some other factor operating here that you haven't found yet. If you find it, five will get you ten you'll have the solution."

Her eyes were steady on me. "That may be true. If you find out what it may be, I will be happy to hear it.

"Now if you will excuse me . . ." She turned to

the rod. I got up and started to leave; as I went out the door, her voice stopped me.

"Charley Judge," she said quietly, "I have one thing more to say before you leave and I continue my duties. Those we talked about, who are marked by strength and ability, by independence of mind and will—you are among the best of them. I value you highly—you and your questions."

I nodded again before I went on. I'd won trophies in everything from nunchakos to marksmanship to most valuable player in the Michigan bantam hockey tournament when I was fourteen. What she had just said reached me more strongly than any of them.

SIX

The palace grounds were encircled by a narrow ring of thick woods. At the outer edge of the woods was a compound, with stables, dairy, cottages, and other adjuncts of the palace.

The armory there was a peaceful spot, smelling of oil and hot iron, shaded by big, smooth-barked beech trees that, after three million years, still looked like those at home in Michigan, except for a bronzy tinge to the bark.

Because of the heat connected with it, much of old Bressir's work was done outside, under one of the beeches; forge, anvil—all his outside equipment and material—could be sheltered from the weather by rolling an awning down an overhead frame. Inside the shop were all the same accouterments and more. Bressir was working outdoors when I arrived, hammering out a hatchet head for some workman. With his tongs he plunged it hissing into a tub of water, then laid it aside and wiped a brawny forearm across his sweaty face.

"You've come for your long sword," he said.

"Right. Is it done?"

He nodded and led me inside. There he reached to an overheard shelf and took the sword down; it

50

was sheltered in a slightly curved wooden scabbard. I drew it and examined it carefully, felt its weight and balance. It was a couple of ounces heavier than the one I had in storage back at Bragg, but it shaved hair from my arm almost as well. Not a Miyaguchi, but good—damned good, for a first product.

"Lovely," I told him. "A fine job."

He chuckled. "What you showed me 'bout making it—it's way stronger for its weight and length than any I've seen or heard of before." He shoved a callused paw at me and we shook.

Then I fastened the sword to my harness, told him to make a couple more, and headed for the guard quadrangle. Ranzil fell out the men not on watch, and I gave them a demonstration with my new toy. Everybody wanted one. Then I drilled them for an hour on the body as a weapon.

It was near noon when I bathed, put on a clean kilt, and sat down to lunch. By that time I'd acquired a squire. Erolanna had sent word to Ranzil to give me an attendant, and he arrived in time to eat. He was a guard apprentice named Farmond, who dreamed of becoming a fighting man. I was his paradigm—super-warrior in the flesh.

I'd have preferred the company of Watchcat, but she had duties of her own. And there were places it wasn't cool for her to accompany me. Like town.

I ate lightly, and watched Farmond eat. At fifteen years, he was about five-feet-six, weighed about one-twenty to my one-ninety, and ate three times as much as I did. I've never been a big eater; my dad, who'd played fourteen years of pro cornerback, used to worry about me not eating enough. And I'd forgotten how much some kids could stow away. When the food was gone, we went to the stable and got our horses.

I'd renamed my horse "Wind." I didn't know how fast he might be, but it was a better name than Groll. And to rename him made him feel more like mine. We rode out of the compound and down a narrow dirt road with pasture on one side and a vineyard on the other.

It felt pretty good to be riding, especially wearing a kilt and proper sword.

I was now in a world where horseback was the advanced and, if you were anybody, necessary form of overland transportation. Horsemanship was taken for granted. So I was lucky to have grown up in a neighborhood where I'd gotten some instruction and experience. Not a lot—I hadn't had my own horse—but at least I wouldn't look like a peasant or a fool. And I intended to practice. While I could ride just fine at a walk—maybe even look all right at a trot or possibly a canter—maneuvering at a gallop or fighting from horseback would be something else.

And I never did like being less than fully competent at anything important to me.

So after a quarter mile to warm him up, I nudged Wind into a trot. After another quarter mile I kicked him into a short gallop. It felt fine, and I let him slow to a canter, then reined him back to a trot.

"How do we get to town from here?" I called to Farmond.

"Turn left when we come to the high road, sire. That's it just ahead," he nodded, pointing. "It will take us there without further turning."

I hadn't been around adolescents much since I was one. Farmond kept watching me admiringly, so I looked squarely back at him. "Where are you from, Farmond?" I asked.

"From a farm in the valley, sire. My father has one of the larger farms; he raises grain and potatoes and beans. He doesn't think much of fighting and war-like ways. But I have two younger brothers to help at home, so when I persisted in my wish to become a warrior, he apprenticed me to the house of the guardian, which has never gone to war or even suffered an attack by brigands.

"But it will get me trained," he added philosophically, "and when I am grown and a belted man at arms, I can take service anywhere I wish. Especially since you are now helping to train us."

The "high road" was better than the side road had been only in having multiple ruts, with no grass growing between them because of heavier horse traffic. We jogged our horses side by side now. A sea breeze ruffled the meadows and pushed small white clouds through a sky that seemed a softer blue than I was used to. Meadowlarks had not changed their song for more than three million years. Kites circled high overhead, watching for dinner.

We came around the side of a small round hill and ahead saw a valley neither steep nor very deep, its river an actual milky blue as it curled its way toward a narrow bay. At its mouth lay a town that might have three or four thousand people. Small sailing ships were tied to its long river-bank wharf. On a hill above the bay was a castle of light gray stone.

I had no labels for the geography here, except for Erolanna's place, which by long tradition was called Amodh Veri. "What do you call the river?" I asked Farmond.

"The Blue River, sire."

Descriptive at least. The milky blue was probably from dissolved carbonates, and the hard stones so abundant in meadow and vineyard were probably chert. Limestone country. There'd likely be caves in the district.

"And the name of the town?"

"Also Blue River, sire."

"What castle is that?"

"It is Lord Cratlik's castle, sire. He is the ruler of this district."

"What's the name of the district?"

Farmond looked startled at the question. "The district of Lord Cratlik, sire."

"And the whole kingdom," I said, "what do they call it?"

"Gel-Leneth, sire. In the olden speech it meant 'fair country,' because it is so beautiful. It is beautiful because the guardian lives here."

The road began angling down into the valley in the direction of town.

"What kind of man is Lord Cratlik?" I asked. "What kind of ruler?"

"Good, most say, sire, and my father one of them. His anger is dangerous and comes easily, and his vengeance is hard, but his taxes are light— only one part in four—and his justice, if harsh, is most often by the law. His personal cruelty seldom touches the farmer, and my father says is more than compensated for by his neither making war nor attracting it to his domain.

Hell, I said to myself, *taxes one part in four? No worse than the U.S. of A.*

The valley bottom was richer and less stony than the uplands. Vineyards were replaced by fields of young grain and what I took to be root crops of some kind. I'm no farmer, but here and there near the river I recognized patches of knee-high corn, probably located for easy irrigation. Men, women, and children were widely visible in the fields, hoeing weeds.

Here the farmhouses were scattered around on their own land instead of being clustered in barrios. They were thatched, and their walls were of flat stones fitted together. Most didn't even seem to be mortared. *Christ*, I thought, *with the limestone around here to make cement from, they should at least be mortared!*

The stab of bitterness surprised me, but then I realized where it came from. *Three million years and more of man, three million years to grow and evolve, and this is what we've come to.* Up till then I could have Erolanna's game—it was okay—but it didn't mean much to me. I couldn't get excited about Juokal's threat to trash the planet. First of all, Juokal wasn't real to me. But now it was starting to feel like my game, too. If I could actually do something to get mankind out of this rut—this was supposed to be sort of a high in this historical cycle—if I could do something about this by kidnapping or killing some budding Hitler or other from out of history, I'd be glad to.

If Cratlik was a good ruler by present standards, what were the bad ones like?

After a bit the road ahead became the town's main street, with the river-bank wharf on one side and buildings on the other. The first building we came to was a stable. In front of it, in a rough wicker chair, sat an old man with an empty sleeve. His eyes were like black marbles tucked behind creased folds. They'd fastened on me from a distance and never left as we approached.

Although I didn't know him, I didn't like him or his ugly smile, and as I drew even with him, I stopped.

"What do you see, old timer?" I asked.

He cackled. It took me by surprise; I thought people only laughed like that in gothic horror tales.

"What do I see? I see—I see a mighty warrior with a strange dark skin." He showed hard bare gums that could probably bite off nails. "And I see—I see a man that consorts with dangerous majickers." He stopped grinning and looked more intently. "Yes. And I see a man who will meet with *great* events soon. *Very* soon. Events which will surprise him *greatly*. Yes."

Then he broke into the cackling again.

I waited, watching, until he was done. There was no humor in his laugh, and in those half-hidden eyes smoldered hatred. I sensed some other things about him now, besides the fact that I didn't like him. One, he was not a seer or clairvoyant. Two, he was dangerous—crazy. And three, he was my enemy.

"Do you know what I see?" I asked him.

His smile turned into a straight slit. "No," he said.

"I see you. I see you clearly and exactly." With that I nudged Wind forward along the street. I could feel those eyes burning into my back as I rode away.

"Do you know that old bastard?" I asked Farmond. He blinked at the word; I made a mental note not to use it here.

"Yes, sire. He is Borkazh, who in his youth was a man-at-arms under Lord Cratlik's grandfather, Lord Gorm. Gorm died of poison, and Borkazh found no favor with the new lord.

"Then he went to fishing for his living, but ill fortune fell upon him and his partner. The fish avoided their nets, and his partner, who'd borrowed to buy the boat, hung himself. After that, Borkazh shipped out as a common sailor. Twice he was shipwrecked. Once he was lost for years—ten years, it's said—and the story among sailors is that he was the only one who survived. Finally he became a woodcutter, and a tree he was chopping fell backwards. It killed a man and his oxen, who were dragging logs, and crushed Borkazh's arm, which the surgeon cut off."

I stopped by a wharf to look over a ship tied there. It looked pretty typical of the several I could see farther on.

"And what do people here think of Borkazh?" I asked.

"They feel sorry for him, mostly, though there are those who dislike and shun him. He earns his bread doing errands for any who bid him, and he lives in the cabin of a fishing boat that was driven ashore and wrecked by a storm."

Something continued to bother me about the old man, and I probed further. "Does he have a son named Lurz?"

"Borkazh? No, sire, he had only one child. Their cottage caught fire one winter night, killing his wife and son and driving poor Borkazh out into the cold."

Poor Borkazh? I thought. *What about his friends? I'm better off having him as an enemy!* It occurred to me that not all "ruiners" were tigers or great white sharks. Some were much smaller. Like rats: they carry the plague.

"Have you ever been aboard a ship like that?" I asked, indicating the tub beside the wharf.

"No, sire. Fishing boats, but nothing big like that."

I slid off my horse. "Let's see if they'll let us on board."

There was only one man aboard, the mate, and he showed us around. This was her home port. Her crew was with family or friends, and the owner/master was ashore making arrangements for a cargo. She was broad-beamed and fifty or fifty-five feet long, schooner rigged, with two stubby masts. Decked her full length, she had a small forecastle and poop and steered with a tiller instead of a wheel.

She was nothing I'd care to ship on, but my knowledge of ships came mostly from books. I suppose she was more fit to sail than anything the Phoenicians or Vikings had, or probably even Columbus.

She did have a hand-operated pump. I couldn't decide whether that was a good sign or bad. Her domestic facilities amounted to two rows of water casks that could be roped snugly into racks amidships, a few wooden buckets, something like a hibachi to cook on, sacks of charcoal in a pile, and a chest of cooking gear.

Three million years of ships had come to this! What in the name of god had become of the knowledge that built *Columbia* and *Challenger*? Or even the great clippers, tall and proud and graceful, that with nothing more than the wind to drive them had carried tea from China to New York in only weeks. I felt like breaking something, or throwing up.

I thanked the mate for the tour and shook his beefy hand; then Farmond and I went ashore.

"I suppose there's an inn in Blue River?" I asked as we got back on our horses.

His eyes brightened right up. "Yes, sire."

"You want to eat?" It was a rhetorical question. "Oh yes, sire!"

It had only been a couple of hours. "Good. Lead on."

We rode another quarter mile and there was the inn. Like the farm houses and almost every other building I'd seen since leaving the palace, it was thatched. But it had two stories, and its walls were both mortared and white-washed. There was a long hitching rail in front; we tied up and went in. There weren't more than nine or ten other customers, most of them looking like sailors.

I ordered roast beef, bread, and beer, paying in advance with some coins Erolanna had given me. The beer was warm, with a heavy malty flavor. The mugs were metal—maybe pewter—and dented, as if some customers had used them as missiles. With them, the innkeeper brought two coarse dark loaves and a crock of what I thought was uncolored butter but turned out to be a soft cheese. After a while, a large hunk of roast beef appeared on a deep platter, in a pool of drippings.

To my surprise, there were forks! We provided our own knives.

I was in no hurry. I wasn't even hungry. What I was was depressed, and wondering whether I ought to raise hell with Erolanna to send me back home. I decided I didn't want to be here, even with her; the whole situation seemed too hopeless. And if there actually was a Juokal, and he trashed the place, I wasn't ready to die.

But then, if I went back, anything I'd do back there would seem empty, because I'd know what a bummer the future was. And I'd know what a cop-out I'd been because I'd given up on what might be a chance to change it.

But what kind of a chance? What the hell good could I do? Erolanna's kidnapping plan didn't seem to work.

And then I wallowed through the whole mental cycle again while sawing off another bite of meat, dipping the end of my half loaf in the juice, and swigging at the beer.

In other words, I was acting like a turkey. Or a

squirrel mentally running on a wheel and getting nowhere. Out of character for me. So I started looking around, to get unstuck. It was time to pull my act together, at least enough to go home to the palace.

Farmond wasn't having a bit of trouble. He was oblivious to my stewing, stoking his lean young belly as if it had been days. The cockroaches, on the other hand, weren't doing so well. The inn had a cat who'd made it her special game to exterminate them. I watched her launch herself from her perch on the bar; the big roach was quick, but he wasn't in her league.

That's when they came in—five of them. I knew immediately what they were and why they were there. I also had a pretty good idea who'd sent them and who'd sent word that I was in town. They were dressed in ordinary working men's clothes, but all carried short swords as well as daggers.

They went to the bar and ordered beer, talking louder than there was any need for. And they kept throwing quick, furtive glances my way.

"Who are they?" I asked Farmond quietly.

He took his attention off the food, and as soon as he saw them, he looked worried. "I recognize only two of them," he murmured. "One is a hoodlum of the town, often in trouble and fights. Very dangerous. The other is Parto, a man-at-arms of Lord Cratlik's, or was, at least; he's not wearing Lord Cratlik's livery now. He's said to be a great swordsman. The other three I do not know."

"Well," I said, "I think there's going to be a fight. I should be able to take all five, with a little luck, if you stay out of the way. So if trouble starts, get to the wall. Go out the window if you need to."

I started to get up and the leader called to me. Or rather, to the room at large.

"Hello? What have we here? A man who lay in the sun too long! Burnt dark as the curst of a loaf! He must be the foreigner we heard of, who beat and robbed a farmer up the valley."

"That's right," said another. "Dark, they said he was, darker than any man they'd ever seen, with hair like short black wool."

"And raped the farmer's wife," said a third. "At knife point. Maybe we should take him down and cure him of that weakness."

"Aye," said the leader, "a fine idea. But if he struggles, kill him. He's naught but a foreigner."

He stepped away from the bar, some thirty feet from us, the others a half-step behind forming a ragged line, with short swords in their hands. I let them come part way, ugly grins on their faces.

How fast am I? I'm not one of the greats, but I've been validated by some who are. I was on the poor suckers before they had time to stop grinning. One head hit rolling, and before its owner began to fall, another head followed it. A third started to raise his sword, and my blade went through arm and chest, taking him almost in two. A fourth fell gibbering to the floor untouched, in a total psychotic break. We were all sprayed with blood.

I backed the fifth to the bar, my sword at his chest. He dropped his own as he backed away, his mouth sagging, his eyes like two boiled eggs.

"Who sent you?" I asked.

He was too shocked to answer until I sliced across his jerkin, laying it open with a thin burning line beneath that oozed red.

"Who sent you?" I repeated.

"Lurz.' The name caught in his throat, coming out little more than a whisper.

"Louder!"

"Lurz." This time it was a croak that everyone there could hear.

"And how did this Lurz know I was here?"

His mouth opened, closed, opened again. "Borkazh," he said.

"And how did Borkazh know to send word to Lurz?"

"Lurz told him to watch in case you came to town, and to let him know at once. Then he arranged with several ruffians in town." He was beginning to babble now, for dear life. "Hort and I were to come down and lead them, to see the job was done. These three—" he gestured at the floor— "were all we could find on short notice."

"And what were you told to do when you found me?"

He swallowed, and I made another slit in his jerkin. "Kill you," he whispered.

"Say it louder," I ordered, "so everyone can hear."

"We were to kill you." His face showed complete despair. He figured he'd bought it with those words.

"And again, who was it that ordered me killed?"

"Captain Lurz."

"And who sent word so you could come down and do the deed?"

"Borkazh."

"Did everyone here hear that?" I demanded without taking my eyes off the man in front of me. There was a general murmur of agreement.

"Did you hear it, innkeeper?"

"Indeed, sire."

"Then take paper and pen and write what I say."

While he got the materials, I killed time making more little slits in the man's clothing. Then I began to dictate.

"Dear Lord Cratlik. A good day to you. This letter is to tell you that you are ill-served by the fool Lurz, who soils your name with his ill service and stupidity. Next, I would like to apologize to you for not killing Lurz when we last met, which would have rid you of an idiot. Also, I hope you will not severely punish the bearer of this letter.

"Sign it, 'your friend, Charley Judge.'"

With some repeating, he got it all down and gave it to me. I looked at the man at my sword's end. "Your name?" I asked.

"Parto," he said. He was looking better.

"Parto," I said, holding up the letter, "I have an order for you. Will you obey it?"

"Oh *yes*, milord."

"Good. Take this letter to Lord Cratlik. Not to Lurz. Do not give it to Lurz or to anyone else, or even mention it, but take it only to Lord Cratlik. Deliver it to his hand. Tell him everything that happened here, omitting nothing. Do not add anything. Do not leave anything out. Tell him exactly what happened, and who sent you to kill me, and that it was Borkazh who sent word to come.

"If you fail in this, in any way, and do not do exactly as I have ordered, I will come after you. You will not escape me, nor will I spare you again." I wiped my blade on his pants, handed him the letter, and gestured toward the door with my head. He backed away, nodding, saying, "Yes, milord; yes, milord," then turned and hurried out.

The other survivor was curled on the floor in an unconscious ball, in a really impressive lake of blood. The spectators, my squire included, all were staring at me. I wish Kurosawa could have seen it. He'd have flipped.

"Let's go, Farmond," I said. I wondered if they

had monasteries on Ixmatl; maybe he'd want to be a monk now instead of a warrior.

As we rode off up the street, it occurred to me: sixteen hours earlier I'd asked myself if I could actually kill anyone.

Erolanna was taking a break, dancing alone in the garden and looking stunning. She stopped as I walked toward her, and her eyes widened. "What happened?" she asked.

"Lurz sent a party of assassins to kill me. It's all taken care of now." I gave her a rundown. "Can you do something for me?"

"What?"

"Show me Lurz in the viewing sphere. I want to see what's going on."

She agreed and I followed her to her study. This time she left the sphere on its stand. It worked fine without her touching it, and there was Lurz. I'd never seen a rack before, but I knew it when I saw it. He was greasy with sweat and gray with pain. Parto must have whipped his horse all the way home, and Cratlik had made up his mind on the spot.

And it gave me exactly zero satisfaction. No, it gave me minus.

Erolanna made the picture disappear from the sphere, but I knew that in the castle above the bay it was still happening.

"You know what?" I said. "Juokal has a point."

She nodded soberly. "But it doesn't have to be the way it is."

"You mean three million years isn't a long enough test?"

"Three million years since the first guardian was given the rod and the sphere," she said gently. She rested her hand on my arm. "Who knows how long this had been going on before that?"

I stared at her.

"But you aren't looking at all the evidence," she added "Did anything good happen today?"

"Yeah. I survived."

"All right. Did anything else happen that was good?"

I looked back. "Um-hm. The innkeeper was polite, and he keeps his place cleaner than I would have thought. And the mate on the ship was a nice friendly guy. Farmond is a good kid; I enjoyed talking with him. I liked working with the troops. And Bressir's a good old guy; he's a pro, with pride in his work. I really like him."

"Ah," she said. "Are people like that worth working for? Worth saving? We do have life. We can use it for something worthwhile."

Her expression when she said it wasn't zealous, or even intense enough to call it earnest. It sure as hell wasn't the noble bit. What it was was matter-of-fact. I decided I really did love that woman.

"Okay," I told her, "you've made your point. I guess we'll just have to hang in there and see if we can handle it. Somebody needs to do *something*. But if there *is* a Juokal and he does something drastic, I still wouldn't blame him."

SEVEN

I set up a routine for myself, starting the next day: work out, train the off-duty watches, ride, lunch, nap, train the morning watch, and read. I didn't know how long or how often I'd be on that schedule, but I would as often as assignments allowed. A routine would help me have time for everything I wanted to do, give me perspective in planning, and make it easier to actually accomplish things.

Reading Ixma was no problem. Written, it was a hell of a lot more sensible and civilized than English. The spellings were not only phonetic, but also there was only one symbol for each sound. They had an alphabet of thirty-six simple characters, and if you could speak and learn the alphabet, you could read.

Erolanna even had a printing press and printer. It wouldn't do to put out the *New York Times* with, or even the *Ontonogon Weekly News*; it was operated by human muscle, using a lever. But it produced printed pages much faster than quill and ink.

I was in the second day of my new schedule, reading in the garden, when Erolanna sent for me.

"I have decided whom you will pick up next," she said. "A woman called Vaarlentia. For a year she was the tutor of young Entomaek, who later would be governess of Africa. Vaarlentia was the origin of a philosophy of government that would eventually collapse one of history's most promising cultures. We will remove her the year before she was appointed tutor."

Right away I didn't like it.

"When was that?" I asked.

"Before present, 2,408,191 years. What is there about it that you dislike?"

I had to look for a moment to spot it. "There's something I want to check first. This didn't work with Wundt. Someone must have filled his place after we picked him up, someone who caused the same effects Wundt would have, so that nothing changed. Nothing important. Let's look and see what happened."

Erolanna considered it. "It may take a little time to locate and identify."

"Start with the obvious," I said. "Check out whoever was the professor of psychology at the University of Leipzig when Wundt would have been."

She nodded and turned to the sphere. It took light and life, there was a short sequence of scenes, and finally a lecture hall, zooming on the man at the lectern.

And it was Wundt! It was Wundt, without any question. I recognized him even in middle age.

"What's the story?" I asked. "Do you suppose the sphere or the rod or whatever didn't incorporate the change in its records after we kidnapped him?"

She was staring even more thunderstruck than I was. "No," she said, "that would happen automatically at the moment of the pickup."

"Well, something's wrong. I brought him up and he died and we buried him. We both saw that."

She didn't answer. Instead, she changed the picture, and there was the young student Wundt in his room again. He listened, put down his pipe, spoke, spoke again, picked up the poker, and went to the door. I pushed my way in, leveled him, and crouched beside the unconscious form. After a few seconds I collapsed across his body, also unconscious.

No one disappeared! Erolanna and I both stood staring. She speeded time within the sphere until Wundt stirred, raised his head, and pushed me off him. Not really me, though; I'd returned here. He pushed what looked like me off of him, knelt beside it, and felt for the pulse, then shook his head.

"*Tot!*" he muttered. *Dead.*

I looked at Erolanna and she at me. She was devastated. Her big hope and project to salvage Ixmatl/Earth and mankind looked blown away. It looked as if the time machine didn't actually take a body from one coordinate and move it to another; it made a perfect duplicate, and then the duplicate died, maybe not so perfect, after all.

But wait a minute, I thought, why hadn't my duplicate died shortly after arrival in Berlin, the way Wundt's did so quickly after arriving here?

I ran through these things out loud, then turned to Erolanna. "When you sent me back, I didn't leave a body here, did I?"

"Of course not," she said.

"You told me you tested this thing. What did you test it with?"

"First with a stone, then with fish in a bowl, and brought them both back. When I sent them, they were gone from here."

"When you brought them back, was anything left at the other end?"

"I don't know. At the moment of return, the connection is broken. I did not reestablish it to see."

"How were the goldfish afterwards?"

"I fed them this morning."

I stood there, buffaloed and exasperated; the equation had too many unknowns.

"Let's try it again. Get the fish."

"No," she said, "goldfish are not humans. It would mean nothing. Being human is part of the difficulty we have witnessed, I am sure."

"Okay," I said, nodding toward the sphere, "set it for the Yukon Flats on January 15, 1987 AD at about 1600 hours. Can you do that?"

"If you will help me access the place. Put your attention on the incident you want to view."

I closed my eyes and did as she told me, then opened them. There in the sphere were eight troopers in white, skiing through upland spruce, the snow like very white flour. I was leading, breaking trail. We hit a little break in the terrain, and I paused to scan out across the muskeg swamp that spread below in the night. Then, one after the other, we glided down the short open slope past little clumps of birch scrub and started across the open flats below.

There in the pleasant warmth of Erolanna's study we could hear an arctic wolf howl three million years away, an unusual bass howl that was nonetheless the essence of wolf, and without slowing his strides, the trooper that had been me glanced up at the sky. And disappeared! Sergeant Holmberg, a dozen feet behind, pulled up, and then the others, closing up the line. They just stood there, staring at the end of my tracks. No one said anything.

They looked around and up, each of them, as if I might somehow have leaped to some point a few dozen yards away or levitated overhead. Corporal Wengert even probed idly into the snow with the handle of a ski pole where the tracks ended.

I shook my head at her, and Erolanna made the picture vanish. So my coming here hadn't been a duplication, but an actual transfer. But without the time "machine."

"How does that thing work?" I asked, pointing at the diagram that was the visible part of it.

"Basically it magnifies—intensifies—my intention."

"Intention!" For a moment I thought she was jiving me, but then I knew better. "What kinds of intentions will it magnify? Can't you just intend it to work the way you want?"

"Not as it is now. It does what it does; it operates through physical laws."

"Well—okay. Then, how do those laws work?"

"I'm afraid I don't know."

I looked at that one gingerly, like I would a cobra wrapped around my leg. "You . . . don't know. Then how in hell did you design it?"

"Intuitively."

"Oh for chrissake!"

I realized I was glaring at her.

"Sorry, Erolanna, I'm not mad at you, just frustrated. And getting hit by too many things that are . . . very, very foreign to me. That's an incredible invention you've got there, and it took remarkable intuition to invent it. Or even conceive of it. I just wish we knew how the thing worked. Then maybe you could tinker it so it did what we need it to do.

"Hell, you probably can anyway, intuitively. Why don't you work on it. I'll go leave you alone."

I turned, left, and went out in the garden. I was starting to feel strange, like something bad was building inside me. I didn't see Diana, didn't care, didn't want to see anyone. I couldn't recognize anywhere to turn next; like the guys I'd left behind in Alaska, I was mystified and helpless.

But it was more than that, because I also felt mean and dangerous. And I was coming down with something. My head was starting to hurt, and I had a chill. My back was beginning to ache. *Shit*, I thought, *that's all I need—the goddamn flu.*

I sat down on a bench. I wanted to break something, tear things up. I couldn't remember ever feeling that way before. Not that strongly.

But I was too weak and sluggish to get violent. Instead, I lay down on the sun-warmed marble and put my forearm across my eyes to keep the glare out. *I really ought to go to my room, to bed,* I thought, then went to sleep there on the bench.

Passed out would be more accurate. Erolanna sent Farmond to check on me; he found me there on the bench and got help to carry me to bed. I didn't even wake up.

After a while I got delirious, soaked the bedding with sweat, raved, jumped out of bed and flailed around and fell down, and never knew any of it. I went through cycles more or less like that for about eighteen hours.

Then I slept soundly for another twenty. When I woke up, I felt too weak to do anything, even walk. I just lay there and let Erolanna's quiet servants do whatever they wanted: prop me up, spoon broth into me, poke bites of fresh melon into my mouth. I drifted in and out of sleep and actually thought very little about anything. Then I woke up from what was half dream and half reverie with the realization of what had turned this all on. I'd stood with Erolanna looking at the sphere, seeing Wundt's room, *and had watched myself die!* Not really, of course; it had been a duplicate with nobody home, but subconsciously I'd equated it with dying. And after a little while it had snuck up and hit me between the eyes.

Just spotting that made me feel better. Moments later Erolanna came in smiling, aimed something at me for a moment that looked like some weird and elaborate crystal sextant, then talked cheerfully for a few minutes and left.

I lay there thinking that I ought to get up, when Watchcat came in.

[Charley Judge,] she thought to me, [will you do me the pleasure of walking with me in the garden? If you are able?]

"Sure, old buddy," I said, and carefully sat up, then got up. I shuffled over to a bench where a clean kilt had been laid out. Farmond heard me from his post just outside the door and came in.

"Where are my boots?" I said. "And my sword?" He hurried out and was back in fifteen seconds. When I was dressed and armed, I tottered off down the hall with Watchcat, feeling steadier almost by the step. Farmond would have gone with us, but I explained that I needed to talk privately with her, that she was my advisor.

In the garden, I sat down on a bench to rest a little in the sunshine. Watchcat sat down facing me.

"Diana," I said, "you are one of my all-time best friends. But I don't know much about you. What do you do with yourself when you're not on duty?"

[I . . . pursue my personal interests.]

"A polite putoff if I ever heard one. That's okay though. Even friends have a right to privacy."

She sat gazing at me like any housecat might, inscrutably. A ninety-pound, beautifully blue and copper-red inscrutable kitty. But she didn't stay inscrutable long. [No, Charley Judge, I will be happy to confide in you. As different as we are, you and I, you are my favorite being.

[My most important personal activity is undertaking to expand my abilities.]

"Such as? Specifically."

[Mentally I go to other places, observing life. It is a source of knowledge and understanding. But there is also the coming and going—the mental exercise of traveling by the mind. Six months ago it was difficult to leave my body for a distance of a few feet and observe it from outside. Now I go freely to other lands. Or worlds.]

I stared at her, trying not to discredit what she had told me, seeing her more sharply and clearly than before. Her large golden eyes looked steadily back, pupils contracted to points in the bright sunlight.

"How do you do that?" I asked. "How do you go on these, uh, trips?"

[I simply . . . leave the body. Without it, I can go almost anywhere. Except in time. I have found it dangerous for me to travel back in time, in the mind. Twice I became very ill, as you just were.

[Fortunately, watchcats do not die easily.]

We got up and began walking the paths through sunshine and shadow, in summer breeze and currents of garden fragrance. Only once, I thought, had I seen Diana upset.

"Why were you so angry when Cratlik loosed the eagle?" I asked. "Did you know it would attack you? I wouldn't think it could have done much to you. If it got close enough to, you'd have had it for lunch."

[My physical injury was no part of Lord Cratlik's intention. The intention was to humiliate me and thus degrade the guardian, of whom he is jealous. I perceived this even as he was removing the hood. If I ignored the bird, it would rake me with its talons, perhaps even blind me. I was thus to be forced to defend myself, to provide a spectacle and be harassed homeward.]

"So he unleashed the eagle on you and Lurz on me."

[He struck at you because you foiled his game with me. At you he was angry, even willing to have you killed if it could be made to appear a fight. But you turned his game around. Yet not to his humiliation; you did marvelously at defeating him without humiliating him. Having struck Lurz, it was the only way you could have survived without at least ugly injury. And you survived with victory.

[You are a remarkable being, Charley Judge, more than you realize.]

"I sure as hell humiliated Lurz though. It can be dangerous to humiliate someone."

[It impressed Cratlik. It was something he could appreciate and admire. Had you simply been physically dangerous, and killed Lurz out of hand, Cratlik would have felt threatened, not intrigued. They would have left you on the ground, bristling with arrows.

[Now Cratlik *is* intrigued, and admires you. He would be very resistive to having you killed. But it is more than admiration. Beneath that cruelty is more boredom than evil, and I believe he hopes for something from you, although he does not recognize this. He hopes for your success.]

"Success at what?"

[I do not know, in truth. But I wish it too, whether

it be at Erolanna's endeavor or some other. You did not arrive here without reason. And I will support you as I can.]

When we finished our walk, I went back and lay down again. Before I dozed off, I thought about our conversation, and about Cratlik wanting me to succeed at whatever I'd come here for. If anything. And about Diana wanting me to.

I didn't feel good about it. Somewhere in there was an unspoken charge, an implication that heavy things hinged on it. As if someone had laid a heavy trip on me, like sending Frodo to destroy the ring of power in Tolkien's trilogy.

But Frodo had purity of heart going for him.

EIGHT

It was a favorite hour of mine—about half dark in the evening. A holdover from playing hide-and-seek when I was a kid. A thrush was still declaring himself in the woods outside the garden wall.

Erolanna wasn't saying much, and I hadn't been either. We were just absorbing the evening. But now something came to me, and I wanted to know.

"Erolanna, today you came to my room with a kind of fancy crystal thing with curls and angles on it. You held it up and pointed it at me. What was that?"

"Ah," she said, "that was an imprint recorder. Come. I'll show you."

I followed her to her study, where again she gestured a lamp into life. Then she picked up another sphere, of about the same size as the viewing sphere but with two crystal rods sticking out to form a vee. She held them like handles, or maybe controls. It lit up like a giant jewel, like a fantastic fire opal but with violets, blues, and greens as well as flame colors.

"The light pattern you see is an imprint," she said, "your imprint, the one you saw me take." I moved closer. "The instrument you asked about takes a reading on the person. It is viewed here in the imprint sphere."

The imprint was a slightly oblong disk of light—a pattern of variegated colors most intense in a distinct core area.

"The nucleus," she went on, "is a unique and unchanging attribute of a person—unchanging, that is, except for size and intensity. For that reason we call it 'the signature.' And this swirly-looking area around it is called the 'halo,' which changes, even greatly, with mood and condition. In this case, it shows a very low energy level and a somewhat depressed emotional level."

It was the signature that intrigued me. It had a pattern like some graceful abstract painting—impossible to describe but easy to see. And beyond and beneath the pattern was a feeling—for me, anyway—like a response to a once familiar picture, long unseen but unmistakable.

The halo was a cooler, paler light, and seemed to flow out of the signature as I watched. But by focusing on given features, I could see that the apparent movement was an illusion; as recorded, it was entirely static.

"And see the sooty zone near the edge?" she asked.

"Um-hm."

"We call it 'the cloud.' It is the usual but not invariable accompaniment of any person. It darkens and lightens, and occasionally, when a person feels a sense of special well-being or emotional strength, it may be absent. It is always strongly present in anger or grief or active illness. That it was not heavy in this imprint told me at once that your illness had truly passed and that you needed only to regain your strength."

She left it there for a moment longer. "And now

this," she said, and abruptly the imprint was replaced by another. "It was yours during the depth of your illness."

I was startled. The signature was not more than half its diameter in the other, and markedly less vivid, although the pattern seemed the same. The halo was darker than in the other imprint, with pattern lines that were utterly different—not flowing curves, but ugly and erratic. The cloud occupied more than half the imprint—murky, with a roiling appearance that made the term "cloud" seem exactly right for it.

"Your cloud," Erolanna continued, "was unusually, dangerously dark. But your signature remained surprisingly strong, considering the heaviness of the cloud. When I saw that, I concluded that you would not die."

"Interesting," I said. "Have you got one of Diana? I'd like to see it."

She looked at the idea thoughtfully. "I have never seen a watchcat's; it never occurred to me. I personally have not played much with the recorder. Animals do not have signatures, not even the finest stallions. They have only a central glow. These things were investigated long ago by the guardian who created the first recorder.

"But watchcats—" she paused—"I believe watchcats would have signatures as humans do."

"Take Diana's sometime," I said. "You might find something a cut above human. Have you got one of you?"

"Yes. It was taken when I was a child, part of my examination as a candidate for guardian trainee."

"What does it look like?"

"I don't know. I have never looked at it."

The sphere changed again, and there was a lovely

imprint, all swirled about with glowing pastels in the most aesthetic patterns. There wasn't the slightest sign of a cloud. But the signature—I examined it carefully—was large and bright, but . . . "It looks just like mine," I said. "I even get pretty much the same feeling looking at it, considering the difference in the halo."

I turned to her; she was frowning slightly.

"No, the differences are there, Charley Judge. They are simply inconspicuous. The signature is a material visualization of the being divorced from the body. Even identical twins have different signatures."

As if to prove her point, she turned to the viewing sphere, calling into it a view of the imprint sphere when it had had my imprint on it. Then she held the imprint sphere beside it to compare the two signatures side-by-side. The only difference I could see was that hers was bigger and brighter, which wasn't supposed to count.

Her frown had changed, was one-part perplexed and two-parts troubled. I didn't say anything. After half a minute, both images disappeared.

"They appear to be the same," she said, then averted her face, rubbing the bridge of her nose absently. "Charley Judge, I need to be alone."

"Sure," I said. "If you need someone to bounce ideas off of, let me know. In the inimitable words of my Georgia daddy, I'm going to go hit the shucks."

The idiom probably didn't mean anything in Ixma, but being telepathic, she knew what I meant.

As I walked to my room, I thought of hunting up Watchcat first. But I didn't really want to talk to anyone just then. On the face of it, what was there to talk about? A mistaken assumption of long standing about the supposed significance and uniqueness of signatures, coupled with a coincidence. Or maybe differences too subtle to really notice. What difference did it make? We *were* two different people, obviously.

I was pretty sure of that.

NINE

Erolanna didn't summon me the next day, and I didn't look her up. I felt stronger than I would have expected, so soon after my illness, and wanted to do physical things. So I went onto my little-used schedule. More or less.

I especially wanted to get out on Wind and explore. Farmond and I got lunches packed and I would sacrifice my after-lunch nap; that would give us about four hours with the horses instead of my scheduled hour-and-a-half.

If Farmond's lunch had been any bigger, it could have eaten him.

Wind turned out to be a pretty appropriate name, after all. Mounted troops in this era didn't wear much armor, and their horses were built more for speed and endurance than strength. And, this time I wore spurs, touching him with them, so that he went into a full run for about three-eighths of a mile, leaving Farmond well behind. Then I reined him back to a brisk trot. It was the hottest day I'd seen here—probably eighty or more—and humid, and I didn't want to overwork him.

Mostly we trotted and walked them intermittently. Exploring the edge of the cliffs, a hundred to a hundred and fifty feet above the sea, we found an old trail that led down to the shingle beach, where we ate.

The tide was coming in but was still well out from the drift left by the last high tide. I knew this had to be the open ocean; a sea like the Baltic or Mediterranean, or the Gulf of Mexico, wouldn't have tides like that, not even with the moon visibly closer than in my time.

I'd never had much to do with the sea, aside from reading about it. Seas were something to fly over. I'd been through the Navy's frogman training—now *that* was heavy duty—but it didn't tell me much about oceans and seas.

"Are there clams to be dug in places like this?" I asked Farmond.

"I don't know, sire. I've heard of clams—townsfolk and fisherfolk eat them—but I've never seen any. Fisherfolk could tell you."

I could understand that. In a culture like this one, a peasant farmer half a dozen miles from the ocean would scarcely have time to go to the beach and dig clams. Setlines and fish traps in the nearest stream would be his style. I'd find out about clams my next time in town.

What I wanted was to do more things with Erolanna—create a broader relationship. Ride out here with her, dig clams, make a driftwood fire, cook them on the beach, and ride home under a full moon. Things like that. Taking her to bed was fine, but I wanted a lot more than that.

Kids, eventually, after she retired.

I wondered if I'd age a lot faster than she would, or if she could apply her magic to me. I wanted to be with her for a long time.

When Farmond had overcome and eaten his lunch, we took a ride along the beach. But in places the high-tide mark reached the cliff behind the beach, so we didn't go far. Then we led our horses back up the trail to the rolling plateau and wandered our way home. I got back to Amodh Veri in time to work with the troops of the morning watch, off post for the afternoon. By the time that was done, my day, on the tail of my illness, had caught up with me. I went to my room and slept.

I'd slept long enough to miss supper with both Erolanna and the troops, when one of her serving girls came in to get me. Erolanna was waiting in the garden, in the early evening. I sat down next to her on a bench, aware that something heavy was in the offing.

"Charley Judge," she said, "I have reexamined our signatures carefully and in detail. I have diagrammed each of them. I am convinced they are identical."

"Um-hm?"

"I believe you are familiar with the concept of reincarnation."

I could see what she was leading up to. It had already occurred to me. "Sure," I said. "It's the idea that when you die, instead of ceasing to exist, or going off to some separate place like heaven or hell, you go to some pregnant woman or something and start over again in a new body. Some religions believed that in my time."

"There are sects today that have the same belief." She was looking across the garden at a flowering tree instead of at me. "I strongly suspect that reincarnation is the explanation of our identical signatures. I believe that I am a later reincarnation of you—that we are the same being in two different lifetimes which, in some strange way, have come to coincide."

She turned to face me then, and our eyes joined.

"Erolanna," I said carefully, "that is an interesting theory. But I don't believe it. It just doesn't feel right to me."

"I hope you are right, Charley Judge. I wish it intensely. Yet it would explain more than the identity of our signatures. It would explain your hearing, and heeding, my call for a warrior such as you—hearing it across a great gulf of time. And it would explain our quick affinity when you arrived."

I shook my head. "That's an assumption on top of an assumption. First of all, I don't believe in reincarnation. If I'd been someone else before I was me, I'd remember."

"Perhaps. I intend to test the concept. Far out on the ocean is a land—a large island—called Dhomes Bodai, the home of the sages. And in that land is a master named Uno Ulao, of whom it is said he remembers who he had been in earlier lives.

"I will send you to him through the time machine to record his imprint. You will also ask him to identify an earlier lifetime of his. I will then send you to that earlier time, to record the imprint of that person, if in fact there is such a person.

"If the two signatures are identical, I will consider that proof enough of reincarnation and of signatures remaining unchanged from life to life."

I sat there looking at her idea. It seemed logical enough, but I was afraid of it. What I was afraid of was that it would support her theory. But it was something to do. And if it didn't prove out, it might defuse the idea that we, she and I, were the same person.

"Okay," I said. "But he may not like having to explain and dispose of my dead body when you pull me back. Even if I tell him what to expect."

"That may not be a problem. The time diagram operates on intention—in the case of a stone or a fish, on my intention only. I suspect that when you were in Wundt's room, you intended to bring Wundt with you. His own intention, on the other hand, was to continue his career in Germany."

"But . . ." I began. She gestured me to silence.

"Unconsciously you may have known that he was not coming through, and perhaps tried to remain with him while at the same time trying to bring him unwillingly through. The diagram may have undertaken to cope with these counter intentions by making duplicates."

She shrugged slightly. "Or perhaps not. It is only speculation—an explanation, not established fact. If, when you return here, you do not leave a duplicate, that is all we will need to know."

"Okay. If you'll show me how to work the recorder . . ."

"It is very easy, Charley Judge. You simply point it, like this—" she pointed it at me—"and intend to record."

There it was again: intention. Intention seemed to be the primary energy in the science of magic.

"Got it," I said. "So all I need to do is go through and record his imprint. You're going to set me down next to him, I presume."

"That is right."

She turned to the viewing sphere and it took life. In it I saw a man who might have been anywhere from fifty-five to sixty-five, sitting at a plain heavy table. A scroll lay on it with two stone paperweights holding a section of it exposed. He seemed to be copying it on another scroll.

"That's him?"

She nodded.

"What's his name again?"

"Uno Ulao."

"Are you also sending me back in time?"

"A little. It is necessary for the transfer. But only far enough, this time, that you are there in daylight."

"Is there any specific message you want me to give him?"

Her eyes were as direct as her words. "Charley Judge, you are stalling."

"You're right." I walked to the rhombus and took a deep breath. "Okay, let's do it."

Again there was the briefest sense of being suspended; then I was standing across the table from the master. He looked up, surprised but not startled. His eyebrows arched.

"Are you Uno Ulao?" I asked.

"I am. Who are you?" He had an accent, but I had no difficulty understanding him.

"My name is Charley Judge."

"Charley Judge." He said it as if he was holding it up to the light and examining it. "How did you come to materialize before me? And for what reason?"

"The guardian sent me," I began. "I'm a fighting man that . . ." This wasn't going to be that easy to explain. I started over.

"Someone who called himself Juokal told the Guardian of Ixmatl that unless she straightened mankind out, he's going to destroy the world. So she decided to remove certain people from history— people who'd had a critical and harmful effect on the past." I went on to give him the rest of the picture. "The reason I'm here is that the question of reincarnation has come up, and we want to check out whether it's real or not. To our satisfaction. She has information that you remember past lives.

"And this"—I held up the recorder—"makes a sort of picture of the basic person, the . . . being that, um, that occupies the body. So if I can just make a recording of you . . ."

I pointed and intended, and hoped I'd done it right.

". . . and thus find out who you feel you were in a past life, I can then go back and record him, too. Then we can compare the recordings. Okay?"

He smiled, a nice, clean little smile. "Your story is most interesting. The guardians have a long reputation as being clever and resourceful. However"—his smile disappeared—"I have some important information which she seriously needs." He beckoned me around the table.

"Do you read?" he asked.

"Sure."

"Good. I have here a partial translation of a scroll. The original was written a very long time ago. Read it and tell me what you think of it."

He unrolled the top of the scroll so I could see the beginning, held it up for me, and I began aloud.

THE SCROLL OF HIDDEN KNOWLEDGE
By Jikan Kulo

The beginnings of the universe and of beings
    are lost in the depths of time. The earliest
    time known was of beings like gods. . . .
My eyes moved down the scroll. *Heavy*, I thought.

And SPEKTHOS came to be called by many
    names. But since the fall of the Terrible
    Empire, he has most generally been
    called *Yough-Kalu*, "Sky Father," al-
    though by that time he himself had long
    since fallen and was a memory only. . . .

For "Yough-Kalu," I thought, *read "Juokal."* And he had long since fallen and was only a memory. Hnh! Paragraph after paragraph fitted the little I knew from Erolanna, putting it into a grim and ugly context. She definitely needed to see this.

> . . . and there Bherk-Kari died, and SPEKTHOS was thereby trapped into the cycle of lives and deaths on Ch'matal.

> And he had never identified himself as *Deiwos*, which in that time and place was the name of god. So people believed that Deiwos continued to watch over them from his place in the sky.

> And Gerthan/Shu-Gwelth, with what he had learned from Bherk-Kari, became a great sorcerer, and made a kingdom for himself, and amused himself with evil. And in time retired in boredom, to sleep for a thousand years

And that's all the scroll had.

"Is there more?" I asked.

"Yes. That is where I had gotten to when you appeared."

I frowned down at the material on the table. There was one thing wrong with it, one thing that didn't fit at all. "Uno," I said, "how come the original scroll, the one you're translating from, how come it looks so new? As new as the translation? You said it was written a very long time ago."

"Ah!" he said, "because it is not the original, but a reconstruction." Beckoning, he led me to a corner of the room and lifted the lid of a large ceramic urn. "Here, I'm afraid, is the original."

I looked in. It looked empty.

"I don't see anything."

"In the bottom," he said. "The dust."

I stared. "The dust?"

"Yes. The scroll is very, very old. It has become dust."

I looked at him, then squinted down into the urn. "You mean it crumbled with handling?" I couldn't even see fragments.

"No no. It was already dust when I found it. So old that the language it was written in is quite different from Ixma."

I could hardly believe he'd said what he'd said. "But Uno, if it had turned to dust, how in hell did you copy it?"

"Reconstructed, not copied," he answered. "And it was simple enough. I put my hands on the urn and contemplated what the writer had written."

I decided that wasn't much wilder than telepathy; I'd just been less prepared for it. "Well, if the scroll had turned to dust, how did you know there was anything there worth contemplating?"

"Ah, that I knew as soon as I saw the urn."

"I kept it beside me as I wrote," he went on, "so I could touch and contemplate it as needed. When I had finished, you can imagine how curious I was to know what it said. Only a few words were recognizable to me: Ch'matal, which clearly meant Ixmatl, and Yough-Kalu, which you already recognized as Juokal. Words of such import tend not to change much over time.

"The next oldest writings we have record of are twelve thousand years old. What I have here is much older. Fortunately the language had not changed too much in the interim."

"Wait a minute," I said, "where I come from, we can't read stuff written seven hundred years earlier; it's a totally different language."

His brows raised like fuzzy caterpillers. "Here it is simple to read things dated three thousand years ago. But even so, it was necessary that I master a sequence of languages."

"All right," I said. "And where was the urn all those thousands of years?"

"In a monastery which preceded this one, buried in the ashes cast out by the volcano. Years ago the old monastery began to be exposed by the washing of winter storms. Four years ago, while poking about, I found this—" he pointed to the urn—"and knew I had a find of great importance."

If the information was as good as it looked, it was important all right. "Uno," I said, "could you and I unroll the scroll and hold it out? So the guardian can record and see it? She's watching us in the viewing sphere—the 'sphere of viewing' that the scroll tells about."

His eyebrows jumped again; he hadn't known we were being observed. "Of course," he said, and we spread out the scroll for an unobstructed view.

"Now," I said, "if you'll tell me who you were in some past life—who and when—I'll go take a reading on him."

"There is only one I can give you. I occasionally see incidents from different past lives, but the only one I can identify is the life immediately before this one. I was the master of this monastery then, also—master Vano Aika—and died sixty-eight years ago in this same building."

"That ought to do for the test," I said. "But before I leave, can I ask you a personal question?"

"Ask."

"What's it like to remember a past life?"

"Much like remembering early years of this one. I do not remember the whole thing; just incidents. It happens only occasionally, when I am reminded of something."

He beckoned me, and we went out onto the balcony. He looked in a direction I took for north, at the flank of a mountain.

"One of the things I remember as the young Vano Aika was a great fire that burned the forest over there," he said, and pointed. "Afterward the mountainside was gray ash, with the black fingers of dead trees pointing at the sky. Now . . ."

Now it was thick and green with tall trees. He had gotten to watch the whole cycle of destruction, rebirth, and maturity of the forest. If it was true. If there really were past lives.

"Uno, I really appreciate all this." I reached out and shook his small, firm hand. "You've been a big help. I hope we'll get together again sometime. But I need to go now, back to Amodh Veri."

He nodded, his eyes bright and friendly. I thought of warning him that I might leave a body there on his balcony, but somehow knew it wouldn't be necessary.

There was a pause, and Erolanna snatched me back.

She sent me back eighty years then, into the bedroom of the sleeping Vano Aika. I got his imprint without waking him and was home again in seconds.

The signatures were the same. But we were actually more interested in the scroll. I reread it over Erolanna's shoulder as she ran it on the viewing sphere.

Heavy. So there wasn't any Juokal; that didn't surprise me. But it told us what we were really up against.

TEN

After we'd read the scroll together, we talked about it for a while. So who or what had communicated telepathically with Erolanna, pretending to be Juokal? There wasn't any doubt in her mind that someone had.

I wasn't all that concerned with the question. To me, the scroll hadn't only defined the situation; it had given us a likely solution. Or at least a good possibility. What I needed to do, as I saw it, was go back and assassinate Gerthan/Shu-Gwelth, the "accursed liar," before he got Bherk-Kari killed.

But she wouldn't go for it, although the only reason she could identify was that using assassination was likely to cost a guardian her powers. I told her that if giving Bherk-Kari more time resulted in a lot brighter history for mankind, her power was not a big price to pay. She got thoughtful at that, and said she'd think about it.

I reached for her then, but she took my hands and gave them back to me. "No, Charley Judge, we are one and the same being, you and I. I am convinced of it now."

I didn't argue. I wasn't so sure, at the moment, that we weren't. And while I couldn't really see what difference it should make—I *was* Charley Judge, and she *was* Erolanna, and we lived and thought and acted independently—I didn't want to hassle her.

So I went to the kitchen, where cook and a helper were scrubbing down, and caught up on the supper I'd missed, having some bread and cheese and melon along with a mug of buttermilk from the day's churning.

I felt lousy. I wondered if I'd ever eat clams on the beach with Erolanna or ride the hills with her by moonlight. Or father her children. I'd never been in love before. I'd had girlfriends, and I'd gotten a bit thick with a couple of them—even wondered if I was in love with them—but nothing approaching this. This time there wasn't any uncertainty about it at all.

And we didn't even have that much in common, except for that goddamn signature. I told myself I was going through what most guys go through a time or two in their teens. Except in this case it was the real McCoy.

Again I thought about looking up Watchcat but decided I didn't want to talk to anyone. Instead, I went to my room. And despite my long nap and the fact that it was barely night, I went to sleep with no trouble at all.

The trouble came *after* I was asleep. I dreamed that I was sleeping and that someone had come into my room. I couldn't see anyone, but I knew he was there. He took hold of me and started to pull. But it wasn't my body he was pulling on—my leg or my arm—it was me! He was trying to pull me out of my body, and I knew if I let him, he'd take it over and I'd never get it back.

So I held on for dear life, because that's what it meant to me.

And then I woke up, and that's exactly what was happening. Someone *was* in my room. I couldn't see him—there was nothing to see—but someone was there, and he was trying to get me out of my body. The only difference from the dream was that in the dream I'd been terrified; now I was mad.

I swore in an undertone and told him to bug off. The sense of malignancy in the room was incredible. And then Watchcat came through the window, snarling. She crouched there a short pounce from the bed, her eyes baleful, her teeth showing white, even in the night. I knew her claws were unsheathed, twenty deadly knives. A hoarse hissing came from her throat.

If whoever it was should win our little wrestling match, she'd be all over him, and he'd lose it anyway.

But he didn't back off, so it was up to me—to me and intention, the energy of magic. Well, intention I had, more of it than he did, so I gave him a blast of it. And he backed off a bit. *Out, you son-of-a-bitch*! I thought, and gave him another shot. I felt dangerous, far more than on the night I got sick. Nobody could get off messing with me like that.

For just a moment the malignancy remained in the room, then disappeared. But he left a thought in my mind, a command to come to him. *Fat chance*, I thought after him, *you tricky mother. And if I ever do, you'll wish your ass I hadn't.*

[Very well done, Charley Judge.]

"Thanks, Diana, I think so, too. And thank you for the backup. What'd I do? Yell or something?"

[There was no outcry. I simply sensed the intrusion, and the nature of the danger. I'm afraid there was nothing I could do except deprive him of his victory, should he have won.]

"Who was it, do you know?"

[No. Someone who departs the body as I do, to wander, but with evil intentions—while he sleeps, I believe—and when he awakes, he does not remember his wanderings. He is a very powerful being, probably with a body that is not human. Those are my impressions.]

"Do you think he'll be back?"

[Hardly. You do not fully realize the power you displayed, at the end. No, he will not be back.]

She turned and hopped to the broad windowsill, ready to jump back down into the garden, turning her head to say good-bye.

"Just a minute, Diana."

[Yes?]

"Do you know what happened today? On my trip?"

[Only that it was important.]

"Let's go down to the garden together, then. I'll tell you about it."

She dropped back to the floor and we left the room together, a boy and his cat.

She didn't give any advice, but she was a hell of a good listener.

And when I went back to bed, I felt strong and confident. More than ever in my life. No one could take me. Whatever the problem, I had the solution: *me*. I might not always remember that, I supposed, but the fact remained.

I slept great.

ELEVEN

I awoke to the sound of thunder in the darkness, and it was *really* dark, much more than before. I'd pulled a cover over me in my sleep, and I lay beneath it feeling alert but relaxed. There was a hard-to-describe sense of deliciousness at the prospect of weather, the way there sometimes had been when I was a boy.

Then a chill gust of wind whipped through the window—the advance guard of the rain invasion. I got up and closed it, then crawled back under the cover and went to sleep to the sound of rain arriving on a multitude of pattering feet.

With the coming of day I donned my kilt and barefoot climbed the spire-like tower at the northwest corner of the palace. One of the most enjoyable things to me is watching storms: monsoon storms in Southeast Asia, a typhoon on Mindoro, the incredible deluges of Cameroun.

A balcony some three feet wide encircled the top. Eighty feet above the garden, it overlooked the encircling woods, giving a rain-dimmed view of the rolling grasslands beyond. The thick gray clouds were heavy enough to account for the darkness, and I couldn't be sure whether the sun was up yet or not. The rain was like a waterfall, an all-encompassing, drenching thickness. Waves of wind came in pulses, driving cold curtains of it to batter the streaming walls and sting my face and chest. I stood there grinning like an idiot. *Erolanna*, I thought, *if you took an imprint of me now, there'd be no cloud. None at all.*

But after a few minutes I began to shiver, went back in and down the stairs. I'd have to work indoors with the troops today. I went to the kitchen, where the cook looked at my wet form in undisguised disapproval. She was grumbling that the boy from the dairy was always late bringing the morning milk when it rained. Furthermore, pointedly, breakfast would not be ready for another hour; she pointed at the waterclock on its shelf. As a matter of principle, I scrounged a cold but spicy sausage and went to a covered patio to work out.

Erolanna found me there doing hand-stand pushups and waited until I was finished before she spoke.

"You have a remarkable body, Charley Judge."

I grinned at her with a touch of malice. "We, don't you mean? I'm you and you're me, remember? So, of course, it's really your body, right? And we wouldn't want to be guilty of narcissism."

Her face became more sober; bleak wouldn't be too far from the word. "Do not be cruel, Charley Judge."

"Cruel? To whom? Myself? I'm talking to myself, right? Isn't what I'm saying the logical expansion of what you decided yesterday?"

She didn't turn and leave, or get mad, or cry. She just stood there looking more sober than ever.

"I guess I made my point," I said softly.

She nodded, still just standing there, and I stepped to her, reached and took her hand. "I didn't really want to hurt you—well, maybe a little—but I wanted you to look, to see."

There was a marvelous simplicity in her words and manner. "I did look and see. Late into the night."

"And what did you see? When you looked?"

"I saw—that I had given an instrument more weight than all the other observations I had made. That you are you and I am me. I do not understand, but that much I know, regardless of the signatures."

She could have seen my relief and gladness without telepathy and half-blind, and it brought a smile to her face. "Would you care to come with me where we can discuss this in seclusion?" she asked.

I grinned back at her. "I'd love to," I said.

"Exactly." She turned, and I followed half a step behind to her sleeping chamber.

Later we went to breakfast, and as we ate, we talked.

"Charley Judge," she said, "I am going to do something that a guardian has rarely done before. The law of the guardian advises strongly against it, although it is not prohibited. I am going to confer with the emeritus guardians. And with their trainees, who should be quite advanced by now, as it is less than five years to my scheduled replacement. They need to know about the scroll, and they may have useful ideas. *Our* game is changing."

"How long will it take them to get here?"

"They need not come in person. Each newly selected guardian, as part of her six-month apprenticeship before assuming her post, creates her own viewing sphere with the guidance of the retiring guardian. And when a guardian departs the post, unless it is in disgrace, she takes her sphere with her to her home district. It is hers until she dies, and at that point loses all power."

I stared at her. "Are you telling me that each emeritus guardian has the power to function as a separate guardian? Why hellfire, Erolanna, after three million years you could have a planetful of guardians! Really! You could have the game won by now!"

She looked ruefully at me, with a touch of amusement thrown in. "Would that we could have. But those who can be trained are few, very few. And there is but one rod of knowledge."

"Only one? Why is that? The law of the guardian? Or don't you know how to make one?"

"The latter. Occasionally a guardian has tried to duplicate it, but to no avail."

"So you're going to use them as advisors, then. What are you going to use me for? Now that you're not worried about Juokal any longer and the urgency's off?"

"Right now I want to know if there is any characteristic in the imprint of ruiners that can be used to recognize them. We know that some ruiners who have had strong historical impact have sheltered themselves in near anonymity, either unknown to us or unrecognized at the time as influential. A quiet wife or mother, even the unassuming secretary or valet of some ruler or economic giant.

"What I will have you do is go back in time and record the imprints of some people whom we can assume or suspect were ruiners."

Erolanna wouldn't have selected him herself, but Iosif Vissarionovich Dzhugashvili was an intriguing figure in the twentieth century. And the political deaths of fifteen to twenty million Ukrainians, Russians, Balts and others seemed to qualify him as a ruiner.

We looked him over in the viewing sphere. Physically he didn't look like much—maybe five-feet-four, stocky but not particularly strong looking, though he may have been thirty years earlier. His face was broad and pock-marked, his big mustache more black than gray.

She tried three time ordinates. The first two found him in conference, despite the early morning hours. Even in the sphere, which showed only the physical, there was a deadliness about him. In his eyes, his smile, and the faces and attitudes of the men with him; they were very, very careful, verging on obsequious. And he saw through them with deadly amusement.

At the third ordinate he was alone in his bed, and we could hear the slow, hoarse breathing of sleep. Outside his door, a guard sat, but inside was only the old butcher himself.

I went to the rhombus and stood, recorder in hand, then closed my eyes to adjust them to the darkness of the target room. I felt like I had felt standing in the door of a plane, waiting to parachute into the Laotian jungle to check out an MIA report. Nervous intestine. Nervous knees. Nervous heart.

There was the momentary sense of suspension again, and I was in the dark bedroom I'd seen in the sphere a moment earlier.

And I *felt* the danger! I began to raise the recorder, and the figure in the bed moved, raised itself on an elbow. The broad face, a pale square in the darkness, was directed at me. One hand had slipped under the pillow. I recorded, and almost at the same instant dropped to the floor shouting *"Now!"*

The pickup and the muzzle flash were simultaneous. It was Erolanna's floor my knees struck, while the heavy pistol slug slammed into her wall;

it was that close. I knelt there with my heart thudding. The old bank-robber/revolutionary-become-dictator had slept with one eye open and a finger on the trigger.

After that we tried to select targets less physically dangerous. There was no shortage. And just for the hell of it, I went back a few weeks and got one of Borkazh.

Besides Dzhugashvili, alias Stalin, I recorded imprints of eleven historical figures. None of the others would be familiar to anyone of the twentieth century, which was just one century out of thousands. Eight of the twelve signatures, plus Borkazh's, shared a common characteristic unfamiliar to Erolanna: the "cloud" did not resemble a cloud at all, but was a solid black ring. The other four had heavy clouds, but they were "cloudy." All had more or less ugly halos.

The unique attribute was the solid black ring. We agreed that we had our quick diagnostic feature for recognizing ruiners.

TWELVE

We felt we'd accomplished a lot, and it wasn't even lunchtime when we finished. So I went back out on the covered patio, finished working out, then watched the rain while I cooled down. It was coming about as hard as before, but the wind wasn't gusting anymore. The sky simply poured.

It occurred to me that the road would be too soft for carts or wagons, probably for several days. I stood there at the edge of the splashing, looking for a way that produce and anything else could be delivered. Horses with pack slings? Maybe a cart with very tall wheels six or seven feet in diameter. There'd have to be a way of loading them; maybe the box could be slung beneath the axle. I decided I ought to see how they already did it here.

Someone was coming up behind me—no threat—and I turned.

"Hi, sweetheart," I said. "Come out to watch it rain with me?"

She smiled. "I like your terms of endearment, but it would be better to save them for greater privacy. They might make members of the household staff uncomfortable."

"Right."

"I came to you now because Watchcat just told me what happened last night. The intruder. You had not mentioned it to me."

"To tell the truth, I was enjoying the storm so much, I didn't think of it. And then we ... got involved with one thing and another."

She was learning to grin, which made me feel very good. She had nice teeth, too. Silently we watched the rain together for two or three minutes before going in to the small dining chamber, where a fire snapped sullenly in the fireplace. One of her girls went in to tell cook we were there. Almost at once she returned with a platter.

"I would not be surprised," Erolanna said, "if your visitor was the same being who spoke to me as Juokal. It would be someone with evil intentions who was also a very powerful sorcerer."

Sorcerer. Someone who knew some of the rules of the game, and how to use them, that others didn't. And used them for evil purposes.

Evil. I'd hardly used or heard the word in my era; the concept had gone out of style. There were just poor misused, misguided victims who couldn't help doing bad things. Well, there were those, all right, though no one seemed to do much about them or for them. Nothing very effective. But now I had definitely faced evil—nice, raw evil. And there was a difference. I considered myself somewhat educated on the subject since the night before.

"You know," I said, "I wouldn't be surprised if it was Shu-Gwelth, the accursed liar the scroll told about. And if the son-of-a-bitch operates at the level of covertly putting destructive ideas into the minds of susceptible people in strategic positions, he could have done a lot of damage in three million years."

She nodded thoughtfully.

"Who's the most destructive force on Ixmatl?" I asked.

Her lips pursed. "In a direct sense it has been Gilgaz Koth, Emperor of the Middle Lands. He inherited a small kingdom, and with the sword and ruthless single-mindedness has conquered a large domain—the largest on Ixmatl. Fortunately, far from here. A million or more have died—those who resisted and many who did not.

"But he is not a ruiner, for I have been able to touch his mind, and he has not warred for six years." She looked at me with her small smile. "He was susceptible to the thought that with organization, efficient administration, and a modicum of justice, his empire could become much richer, and he with it. For the last four years that has been his game.

"So I am sure that Gilgaz Koth is not Shu-Gwelth. A likelier one is Lord Urigwerm, the greatest sorcerer on Ixmatl and the ruler of the Inner Sea."

"I'll tell you the truth," I said. "I still think the best way to handle the situation is for me to go back and kill Gerthan/Shu-Gwelth before he betrays Spekthos/Bherk-Kari. The way the scroll tells it, Bherk-Kari was doing pretty damn well until Shu-Gwelth got him killed. Give Spekthos another ten years as Bherk-Kari, or maybe even four or five, and the game might have been won. You've had time to think about it. What do you say?"

"No."

It was a flat, absolute "no." It didn't mean "I don't think so" or "probably not" or "unless you talk me into it." It meant *no*. While *my* pitch, I realized, had almost been an invitation to refuse, full of "I think" and "maybe" and "how about it?"

"First of all," she went on, "we have no assurance—not even a probability—that it would give him five or ten more years. What other ruiner might have been waiting to destroy him? It would change history, however, and somehow I fear it would result in the scroll not being written. And if Bherk-Kari did not succeed, we might then find ourselves in much the same predicament we are in now, without the vital knowlege that the scroll has given us. Without knowing the goal. Without knowing what we must accomplish to salvage mankind from the trap we are in.

"And finally, Shu-Gwelth must still exist as someone else. Someone very powerful, probably retaining the evil purposes which drove him then."

"If that's true," I answered, "then Spekthos must be around somewhere, being someone, too."

Erolanna considered, then dismissed the matter for the time being. "Go work with the guards if you'd like," she said, arising from the table. "I'm going to contact the emeriti and tell them what we have learned and done. I'm sure the *Scroll of Hidden Knowledge* will interest them greatly, Charley Judge. And so will you, when I tell them about you."

THIRTEEN

Funny thing about the sphere: it was only about fifteen inches in diameter, but it seemed, when you looked into it, as big as you wanted.

I'd asked to look the country over before she deposited me there, and she'd agreed. Attuned to my responses to what I was looking at, she directed the view here and there, down and up. Somewhere below would be Bherk-Kari and his students, probably with a crowd around them. Somewhere down there, death waited for him, an ugly, painful, terribly degrading death.

But we weren't looking for Bherk-Kari just yet.

The valley was ten or a dozen miles wide, between low mountain ridges that still, on rougher ground, bore the weathered stumps of past forest. Now cattle, and in places goats, grazed the open, erosion-scarred slopes.

A large river, two hundred yards across, curved its way down the valley through a mile-wide flood plain, carrying on its scintillant back a traffic of small barges, boats, and lumber rafts.

The flood plain had no significant buildings. Any built there would be washed away by the seasonal floods. It was an irregular mosaic of rice paddies, interrupted at intervals by now-dusty roads leading to the river. There were rickety wooden flumes, carried on low trestles of lashed poles, bearing water to the paddies. Tall water wheels turned slowly at the shores, driven by capstans around which oxen trudged, tip-buckets splashing into ramshackle troughs that fed the flumes.

The entire irrigation system looked like something that could be and was taken down and hauled away each year in advance of the flood season.

Back of the flood plain, the land rose abruptly fifteen or twenty feet to a natural terrace above the floods. On it spread fields of grain, beans, and crops I didn't recognize. There were numerous small villages where farmers lived—clusters of huts with occasional larger dwellings. Back of the first terrace lay a sequence of older terraces, becoming less distinct with age and distance from the river, marking the history and progress of the river cutting its valley through the millennia.

And everywere were people, stooping shin-deep in the paddies, bent over hoes in fields, bustling in the villages, or sharing the roads with rude two-wheeled carts and the oxen that drew them.

But it seemed scarcely more primitive than the time I was in. And the people moved with a freedom of motion. They did not plod, most of them; they strode! There was a swing in their movements, suggesting plans and intentions.

In Erolanna's time I had not seen that. The people I was looking at were busy living. Three million years later, most of them would be putting in their time, waiting to die. Those plans and intentions had been defeated too thoroughly, too many times.

Erolanna raised the viewpoint, moved it up the valley as if piloting a silent plane. The bordering hills grew taller, until, in the distance ahead, we could see it narrow, and the ever taller mountains wrapped around it, now dark with forest.

"Let me see the palace," I said, "where Bherk-Kari gets killed."

And abruptly we were there, above the lower valley again, not many miles from where it opened onto an extensive plain. The palace occupied the top of a broad, low hill. Built as a fortress, its walls were thick, probably of packed earth faced with stone blocks, crowned with battlements and cornered by squat, round towers.

But time had brought security. The slope outside the walls had been planted, converted to gardens with flowerbeds, banks of low shrubs, flag-stoned promenades, and occasional fruit trees.

"I guess it's time to find Bherk-Kari," I said.

She nodded, and we were at the foot of one of the bordering ridges, below a canyon that opened onto the sloping margin of the valley floor. A creek rattled out of it, occasional poplar trees guarding its banks. A hundred or so people, followers of Bherk-Kari, squatted quietly in a semi-circle, waiting. They faced a small separate group wearing robes, standing in the shade of a tree. One of the group would be Bherk-Kari, another Gerthan/Shu-Gwelth.

Erolanna reversed the view. A crowd of perhaps fifteen hundred or two thousand were striding across a pasture toward those already gathered, the distant palace visible behind them. Again I was impressed with the energy shown; it contrasted so strongly with what I was used to, in Erolanna's time or even my own. The game was much younger then, the guardians confident, and Deiwos still spoke to man.

Then I was looking close up at the nine men in

robes, and focused on one who, by the intention of viewing, had to be Gerthan/Shu-Gwelth, a handsome dude with black eyebrows and lots of curly auburn hair. My mission was to record his imprint—his and Bherk-Kari's.

"Are you ready?" Erolanna asked.

I nodded. I was dressed in a loincloth like the locals, and unarmed; civilians here carried no more than a knife, if that. With the recorder in my hand, I stepped into the rhombus.

And into a different, vibrant scene, stumbling briefly, then striding with the crowd. No one noticed my sudden appearance on their fringe; their attention was ahead. I could feel them, their intense interest. They *knew* this man was special, this experience important, the knowledge vital that they sought. And I was swept along with them, emotionally as well as physically, eager myself to hear him.

Those in the lead reached the semi-circle of followers already there, and stopped. The rest of us crowded up. Out on the edge, I knelt. Others were lowering themselves, squatting or sitting. I raised the instrument to my eye, aimed it at Gerthan/Shu-Gwelth and then at Bherk-Kari, and my mission was complete. But before she could pick me up, I edged farther into the crowd, as if to hear better but actually to make a pickup awkward. I didn't want to leave yet.

Bherk-Kari stepped forward and began to speak, and the crowd was instantly silent. I didn't understand a word, but I could *feel* his power. Godlike wasn't far off the mark. I didn't understand a word he said, but just listening to his voice made me feel strong and eager.

When he was done, he turned and walked a little way back in the canyon with his students, where they built a fire to cook their meal. The hundred or so followers built fires, too, of dry cow chips and opened little cloth-wrapped bundles of food. Some of the crowd I was with got up and started back toward town, me with them, not walking as rapidly as before, digesting what they had heard, talking quietly. I walked off to the side by myself, and suddenly was in Amodh Veri again, with Erolanna.

"I wanted to hear him," I explained, "there in the flesh."

"Of course."

"Bherk-Kari was more powerful than we realized. He really might have pulled it off."

She didn't answer, but her eyes were steady on mine. She knew what I was thinking: I wanted to knock off Gerthan/Shu-Gwelth.

"If nothing else works?" I asked.

"If nothing else works."

"Finc," I said. "There's one thing more I want to do back there."

"What is it?"

"I want to record the imprint of the king."

"Why?"

"I'm not sure. It'll come to me."

She frowned at the sphere, concentrating; I stepped to her side. A burly man, overweight, walked down a corridor with three attendants, standing out among them by his carriage as much as his vivid indigo robe and gold circlet. We followed him to a private chamber, part of a suite. Two of the attendants stopped at a door, bowed, and continued down the hall. The other, an adolescent, took his robe and circlet to put them away.

The view changed to darkness, broken only by faint light entering through windows. There was a bed, and a bulky body beneath a light cover. *Well, I thought, here we go again. Another bedroom.*

I stepped into the rhombus, went through, recorded and was back. In seconds.

"I want to see it," I said. "King what's his name."

"Wlkwos," she said. "His name is Wlkwos." She got the imprint sphere and called up Wlkwos's imprint. We looked at it and then at each other; the signature was one we knew.

"Uno's," I muttered. "Uno Ulao's."

We compared; there was no question. The signatures of Uno Ulao, the translator of the scroll, and Wlkwos the impaler, were identical.

FOURTEEN

Wlkwos's signature was the only surprise. Gerthan/Shu-Gwelth's imprint had the characteristic black ring associated with ruiners. And Bherk-Kari had a beautiful imprint with a marvelous halo. It did have a noticeable cloud, though, and the signature was unfamiliar.

But it was Wlkwos's that had our attention. His cloud was strong and roiling, his halo not really ugly but unpleasant.

"I felt sure, when I was with him, that Uno was okay," I said. "I've always been good at sizing people up, and I really liked him. Maybe he wasn't Wlkwos. Maybe it's coincidence."

She shook her head. "It stretches coincidence too far."

"Can we trust the scroll then? If someone like that translated it? For all we know, the dust in the urn could have been someone's pickle recipes."

"There is too much truth in the scroll. And people change; beings change. Possibly ruiners do not, but others do."

Erolanna walked over to the viewing sphere, and I followed. Its glow appeared, and there was the urn in Uno's room. Then the room was replaced by blackness, then a narrow valley with forest and a mountain stream. The forest changed but the valley was the same, changed again, and again, and suddenly the forest was gone. A building stood there, two stories tall, made of large bricks. Nearby was a group of outbuildings—a large privy, sheds, a barn—and behind them, a large garden, small fields, a pasture fence made of rails.

The main building must be the old monastery, I decided, the brotherhouse where the urn had been found. Before its burial by volcanic ash. It was not large. A single-storied wing extended out, as if an addition, with narrow windows regularly spaced. It would be a dormitory.

"What was the writer's name?" she asked.

"Jikan Kulo."

The view changed to an interior, where a husky, bald-headed man in a robe was watering potted plants. "That is him," she said. "I want you to obtain an imprint of him. Asleep. I do not want him disturbed by anything startling."

"All right. But first I want to see him finishing the scroll."

She nodded, and the picture changed again. A monk was seated at a table, writing with a quill. Jikan Kulo; but I had to look twice to recognize him, even with the bald head. His body was wasted, his face sunken, and he sat on a pillow. But his expression was intent.

"That's him all right. Find him asleep and I'll go. Get him the following night."

The view became a tiny cell, moonlit through a narrow window, with a low shelf for a bed. A form lay curled on its side beneath a blanket. I went to the rhombus, and in a moment was standing at the foot of the shelf.

I could smell deathly sickness, sour and heavy.

Before I raised the recorder, an arm groped out from the cover toward a bucket on the floor, and the man was sick into it. When he'd finished retching, he laid his head down again, moaning quietly.

I took the recording and got out of there.

"Jesus!" I said to Erolanna, "you can't imagine how bad that place felt. The man is dying. Can you get a date on that from the rod?"

"Of course."

"And one on the eruption?"

She picked up the rod.

"I want to know how long it was afterward before the place got buried."

She frowned slightly in concentration. After a few seconds she laid the rod down and turned to me. "Four days," she said. "Why did you wish to know?"

"I'm not sure," I told her. "But you know why he was sitting on a pillow, don't you?"

She shook her head, then her mouth framed an "Ah" as I made a thought of my knowing.

"That's right," I said. "Hemorrhoids. The poor son-of-a-bitch has got a terrible case of piles, I'm sure of it. And I'll bet I know what he was sick with, too. The emaciation, the vomiting—he had a severe bleeding ulcer that turned into peritonitis. He'd probably been hanging on well after he should have been dead, trying to finish the scroll."

She looked concerned. Not because of what had gone on with Jikan Kulo a long time before, but because of the rage that was building within me. It was a lousy, crummy, shitty game.

"And how did Wlkwos kill Bherk-Kari?" I demanded. "He shoved an iron rod up his ass and into his guts, and hung him out over the castle wall to die."

Even a complexion as light as Erolanna's can go pale. We checked Jikan Kulo's signature, and it was the same as Wlkwos/Uno's, exactly as we knew it would be. Then I went to the kitchen and got a bottle of wine; the mood I was in, cook kept her mouth shut and avoided looking at me. I—Erolanna and I—we were going to bust this game of Weirro/Earth/Ixmatl. But first I needed to ride out this rage I felt.

So we got tight, the first time ever for her. After that she went to sleep. I went out and rode Wind long and hard, alone.

Erolanna set me down on the balcony outside Uno's room so I could walk in on him more or less normally. A dove cooed in a nearby tree, and something very fragrant was in bloom. The sun was in the west, marking late afternoon.

When I stepped in the door, he was looking up at me, smiling, expectant.

"Good evening," he said. "I felt your arrival."

That was interesting. If people could feel me arrive, we'd have to be more careful. I didn't want any more receptions like the one in Stalin's bedroom.

"What did it feel like?" I asked. "When I arrived. What was the phenomenon?"

"A sense of presence where, an instant earlier, none had been. I am . . ." he smiled, "perceptive. Even most of the brothers here would not have noticed."

"Do you know what I'm here for?"

He got up and went to an urn, a different, much smaller urn, removed a scroll, and partly unrolled it on the table. "It is done," he said.

I found where I'd read to before and proceeded from there.

. . . became a great sorcerer, and made a kingdom for himself, and amused himself with evil. And in time retired in boredom, to sleep for a thousand years and take another body, and pursue his evil purposes in the game of Weirro/Ch'matal.

The ending of the game cannot be foreseen, for the future is subject to the decisions and actions of the players. But the time will come when the state of mankind is so degraded that even its renascences will be squalid. And the Guardians themselves will be threatened again with destruction.

In that time, mankind will approach the bound beyond which there can be no recovery, but only a doom of permanent and everlasting grief and misery.

And in the time of that dangerous approach will be a last chance for mankind. And those who were principal players in ancient time shall gather again, in fellowship or enmity, to settle their fate and that of all other beings in the game. And these others shall be not only those acting as living humans, but also those bereft of human bodies, who have housed in vermin or cattle or stones, or the bones of the past.

And from that forgathering will come the end of the game of Weirro/Ch'matal. And the end may be a beginning—the renewal of old knowing and ability, and the start of a truly golden age. Or the game may simply grind to a halt, leaving its players mired and lost forever.

I gave the last two paragraphs a second look, and chills ran over my skin. "Shall gather again, in fellowship or in enmity," I repeated aloud, and looked at Uno. He looked back at me with a cherub's bright smile.

"I am ready to play the game to the finish," he said.

"Are you? On which side?"

He blinked at that, his smile faltering. "Why, on the side of Spekthos, of course." He gestured at the scroll. "I have already begun, by providing that."

"Maybe you began before that. You said you could remember things from before Vano Aika but couldn't identify who you were. How about Jikan Kulo? Do you think you could have been him?"

He went thoughtful on me. "It would certainly explain a great deal," he said, "digging in just the right place, being able to sense the contents of the scroll, writing it in a language unknown to me . . . Yes, it seems very possible. Even probable."

"Okay," I said reasonably, "so look at it and tell me whether you were or not."

He looked and shook his head. "I simply do not know. Why are you asking me this?"

I didn't want to verbalize it, even mentally. I wanted him to find out himself. Instead I asked him, "How far is the old monastery?"

"Not far. Less than two miles."

"Will you take me there?"

"Why—yes. Of course." He knew I was testing him, and he wanted to pass.

After taking a moment to roll out the entire scroll for the viewer, we went down to ground level and across the grounds, passing several brothers as we went. Without exception they nodded respectfully to Uno—sort of a head bow—and glanced at me, but he made no introductions. I

expected him to have someone saddle a pair of
horses for us, but we strode off on foot, down a
path through fields where other brothers labored,
and onto a forest trail that followed along near a
small stream.

It was beautiful, pristine as hell, through firs
and ferns, and pines with cinnamon bark. The
only sign of man was the slender footpath, shared
no doubt by wildlife, and the occasional windfallen
tree whose branches had been lopped off so it
could be stepped or clambered over.

Suddenly, in front of me, was a grove of red-
woods rising like towers, probably three hundred
feet or more tall and ten or fifteen feet through.
Dhomes Bodai, an island on the Mid-Atlantic Ridge,
was a long way from California. Obviously, at some
time since the island had formed, man had risen
high enough to travel back and forth between con-
tinents and do things like introduce plants from
one part of the world to another.

Not only would technology have been higher
then. Things like hope, interest, purpose, would
have been stronger then, too.

Minutes later we were at the old monastery.
There was little enough to see—some rubble of
brick walls tucked among the trees, with a couple
of sections intact sticking a foot or two above
the ground. This was young forest—saplings and
small poles—with scattered old snags like silver
pillars amongst the greenery, most of the char
weathered off. A fire had burned here maybe twenty
years earlier, baring the soil, and winter storms
had washed away the old volcanic earth from part
of the ruins.

Uno took me directly to the room where the urn
had been. Actually there were only the lower courses
of bricks, the outline of the walls, with some of the

rubble and dirt thrown out of the inside. He hadn't simply "found" the urn; he'd dug for it.

I thought I knew the room; small, cell-like, it would have had a shelf for a bed and a narrow window about there. I'd been there the day before, or twenty thousand years before, depending on how you wanted to look at it.

"So this is it," I said.

"Yes."

I nodded at a low heap of rubble and dirt. Dirt that had begun as volcanic ash, then been altered by humus and percolating rain, the growing and dying of roots, by freezing and thawing and the comings and goings of worms.

"Sit down," I told him. He sat, and I lowered myself onto another heap, wondering what I was going to do next. I'd have to feel my way into it.

"Pretty remarkable that Jikan Kulo could write all that, eh? When he said 'hidden knowledge,' it had *really* been hidden. Incredible that he could know all that."

Uno nodded. He wasn't as talkative as usual; he was a little afraid of what was going to happen.

"I checked out some key parts of the information on the scroll," I went on. "It's quite accurate so far."

"Yes, I am sure it is."

"Just about as remarkable as you finding and reconstructing and translating it. Even for a master, that's got to be something that would hardly happen once in a million years. Or three million."

He didn't even nod. He didn't look too well.

"Do you suppose Jikan Kulo died in the eruption?"

He shook his head.

"Does that mean he didn't? Or that you don't know?"

"He died in this room."

"Ah! You found his bones then?"

He shook his head again and swallowed. "He died before the eruption, and the brothers had buried him."

"Got it. How do you know that?"

He shrugged his shoulders.

"Okay. How long before the eruption? A month? A year? Ten years?"

"Two days."

"Um. What did he die of? Can you get that for us?"

His face was the color of wood ashes, pale gray, and he swallowed again. I wondered if he was going to be sick.

"Bleeding," he said. "He died of bleeding from the stomach. I can feel it. In the room."

"I see. You feel things from the room, or from the urn. You don't simply remember or feel them from a past life."

A tear brimmed out of one eye.

"Were you Jikan Kulo?"

He nodded. The tears began to flow, and then the words. He told how Jikan Kulo had died in the night, and how the brothers had buried the body the next day with one eye over their shoulders at the mountain. How he, a spirit now, had tried to get someone to open and read the scroll, but they were deaf to him. One had picked up the scroll but, instead of opening and reading it, had put it in the urn with other of Jikan Kulo's personal belongings.

Their minds had been too much on the ground tremors and the steam venting from the flanks of the peak above them. Later that day they had bundled their most portable possessions and left.

"And does all that come to you from the room?" I asked him. "Or do you remember it?"

He was looking better now, but not all that well yet.

"It is my own remembering," he said. "But being here in the room helped to start it." He stood up. "Let us go back now. We will miss supper."

"I've got more questions first," I said. I wasn't sure what they were, but I'd been doing pretty well winging it so far.

He nodded resignedly. "Down by the stream then. This place is oppressive to me."

"We'll stay here," I said. "It's the right place— right for me and right for you." My intention was strong, and after a brief hesitation he sat down again.

"Pretty remarkable that Jikan Kulo could come up with all that knowledge."

He nodded mutely.

"What do you suppose drove him to that? I mean, no one else ever did anything like that. Actually, that's more remarkable than finding the urn and reconstructing the scroll. Don't you think?"

He didn't even nod.

"Do you ever have piles?" I asked. "Hemorrhoids?"

His startled eyes jumped sharply to mine, then dropped. So I had the string now; all I had to do was keep pulling it.

"Do you?"

"Recently," he said.

"Do you people believe in karma?"

"We are familiar with the doctrine. We do not adhere to it."

"Ah. Sometimes karma operates through a sort of—a sort of self-inflicted retribution, isn't that so?"

"It can. Theoretically."

He sounded a little waspish now, resistive to going any further. I had it, all right.

"Okay. Are you aware that, when you wrote the scroll, you never put down the name of the king who had Bherk-Kari impaled? Did you realize that?"

His face went blank. He shook his head.

"What do you suppose his name was?"

He shook his head again.

"Okay. Let me ask a different question then. Were you alive in those days? When Bherk-Kari was teaching?"

His voice was small, the waspishness gone. "I must have been."

"Do you suppose you saw Bherk-Kari die?"

"It's possible. I don't know."

"All right." I raised my voice a notch, putting the words out strongly but without any hostility. Like Perry Mason in the old TV show. "Who were you then?"

Once more he shook his head.

"Okay. Take a look. See if you have a mental picture, from back there."

His eyes focused out past me at something. He looked *bad*.

"What do you see?"

His throat moved in a dry swallow.

"What do you see?" I repeated.

"A man," he answered, "naked, impaled on a metal rod."

"Ah. Whose eyes are you seeing it through? Who were you?"

His face folded, crumpled, like wax melting; then he burst into violent sobbing, tears of terrible grief. When, after several minutes, he could talk, it was in segments, as the long-forgotten past came back to him. Yes, he'd been the impaler. And after Bherk-Kari died, terrible things had happened to him and his kingdom. Then the accursed liar had appeared to him in a vision, laughed at him, told him it had been a lie, that Bherk-Kari had not wished him ill, would never have incited revolt. That Bherk-Kari had been Deiwos—God—who had come down to Earth to save man. And now he was dead.

After that, Wlkwos had hanged himself, and when life was gone from the body, he stayed with it, spinning slowly below the rafter for the bleak, desolate hours before it was found and cut down. And waiting, he'd known that only bodies die, that he could not escape his guilt in death, that he would have more lifetimes.

Uno took a deep breath, his eyes steady on me now, his voice thoughtful. "At that point," he said, "I vowed to myself that I would make up the damage I had done. Somehow. Someday."

His voice became almost conversational. "As Jikan Kulo, I was given to trances, as brothers sometimes are. Even without fasting, I would see visions, hear voices. And then, over a period of weeks, I began to fail rapidly in health, sometimes suffering great pain in my belly and bowels. I had many realizations, writing them down, until at last I organized them all on the scroll. And died."

He smiled then, a smile that was perhaps rueful but not sad. "And in this life—in this life I was careful not to look at the truth so directly; I would not be so foolish as Jikan Kulo: I would not *know* those truths again. I would find them as an interesting relic, as someone else's words and truths, not mine." He chuckled. "Even in someone else's language, and translate it as something that had nothing directly to do with me. I would make them available as an interested bystander."

He stood up. "Let us go," he said. "It is better to be back before dark. You do not have your sword, and sometimes there are wild dogs."

As we swung down the trail and the ruins disappeared among the trees in the beginnings of dusk, he made his final comment about the affair. "It has been said that time heals," he said. "The truth is that time only conceals."

That, of course, was just part of the truth.

FIFTEEN

Erolanna had watched the whole affair, of course. When I got back, I was still full of it; in its way it had been a heady, if heavy, experience, guiding Uno into and through what he had told me. But her attention was on the scroll, and she had not had a chance to read it, so I stood by her and we read it together in the viewer.

"This returns some of the urgency," she said.

"Right. You know what? We need to send me back to just before the game began and bring back a copy of the agreement. The accursed accord."

"I do not believe there is a physical contract," she answered, "something you can bring back."

"Why not? Seems to me that anything that important and that binding would have to be in writing."

"With beings such as we seem to have been, I believe the intention of agreement, however private, would be binding."

"Okay. Then send me back to learn what I can. I'll play it by ear, like I did with Uno. Just send me back; I'll pick up something useful."

She shook her head. "You would if anyone could," she said, "but I can only send you where the sphere

125

sees. And the sphere sees no further than the rod of knowing reaches—to the time of the first guardian. I have no way to send you further back than that."

"*Find* a way," I said. "I don't think you realize how good you are. Look what you've already done: you conceived of and built the time diagram—and even without it you reached back three million years to call me here."

"And you came," she answered. "That is the greatest magic of all. Together we are a force whose potential is just beginning to show." Her voice became reflective, and she recited from the scroll. "'And those who were principal players in ancient time shall gather again, in fellowship or enmity.'" She focused on me again. "So far there are you and me. And Uno Ulao. Who is missing? Who else in fellowship? Surely there will be Spekthos/Bherk-Kari. But in what guise? What beingness in this life?"

"Maybe he's one of the emeritus guardians," I suggested. "Or one of their trainees. Does any of them seem to you like a possibility? How did your meeting go with them the other day?"

"They were very interested. But none advised me; I do not expect they will, unless one of them has a major understanding. Emeriti are not to intrude into the affairs of a posted guardian except under the most compelling circumstances. They did not say a great deal; none of the trainees spoke at all, beyond an introduction.

"But I do not believe any of them is Spekthos."

"Well then," I said, "who's the Good Witch of the South around here? Not counting you."

The reference threw her for a moment; Dorothy and Oz had not survived these three million years. "Who besides you is a powerful magician and uses it to benefit people?" I amended. "That might be a lead."

"I wish I could name one," she said. "Or better yet, several. But in these benighted times there are only two magicians who could be called powerful. One is the guardian. Even the emeriti are not powerful, although they are effective in their own locales and do much good. Being divorced from the rod, and from Amodh Veri itself, is to lose much.

"The other, and perhaps the greatest, is the sorcerer, Lord Urigwerm. And he operates without the aid of rod or sphere. But he is surely a ruiner, far more likely to be Shu-Gwelth than Spekthos."

"And maybe Spekthos isn't powerful anymore," I said. "What happened back there with Shu-Gwelth and Wlkwos—that was a real bummer for him. He came down to save man and ended up impaled. How did the scroll put it? He was 'thereby entrapped into the cycle of lives and deaths on Ch'matal.' He may have spent the past three million years as a wino."

I could see the idea was new to her. After a moment she said, "Perhaps. But the power resides in him still. He was outside the accord; he never agreed to play."

"The hell he didn't. He agreed by coming down and joining in. A matter of intention, like you just said."

She looked at that. "No," she decided. "When Bherk-Kari traveled and taught, he knew who he was and what he was doing. He was outside the accord."

"But after he died—" I said, "crash! He lost it."

She got up, looking tired and a little grim, and walked to the rod lying on the table. "I will find the imprints of the emeriti and their trainees, and compare them with those of Spekthos/Bherk-Kari. Then I will contact them and show them the completed scroll.

"Tomorrow we will examine the possibility that Lord Urigwerm is Shu-Gwelth. But I fear that getting his imprint may be dangerous—more dangerous than recording that of the man who shot at you."

If it's any more dangerous than that, I thought, *I'll be in trouble.*

SIXTEEN

Urigwerm's castle was probably the most impressive structure on Ixmatl. Not the most beautiful; Amodh Veri was. But impressive: a massive structure of great basalt blocks, probably cut while leveling and tunneling the great rock it stood upon. Cornered by dark, round towers and topped by battlements, it was a single building crowning a great volcanic plug that thrust its head out of the sea. Impossible to scale without rock-climbing gear, it could have resisted anything short of an airborne assault or a prolonged bombardment by heavy naval guns. Outside of nuclear attack or biological warfare.

I could see two small ships riding the hook near it. There had to be some way, short of magic or being born there, of reaching the top. Not that that would be a problem for us. We'd simply bypass all that and deposit me inside with the time machine. I'd get the recording and zap! Back at Amodh Veri again.

"Lord of the Inner Sea," I said. "What does he do out there? Besides admire the scenery?"

"There are rich lands around the Inner Sea, and much commerce on its waters. At its eastern end its waves wash the shores of the empire of Gilgaz Koth, and Urigwerm extracts tribute from them all. His storms founder any ship from a ruler or merchant who does not pay or tries to cheat."

"His storms? Are you saying he controls the weather?"

"He can make a sudden squall arise, sufficient to overcome any ship. What sailors call a white squall, which strikes without the warning of any storm clouds. He uses these and, by report, certain creatures that live in its waters, to ensure payment and the respect of fear."

"Let's have a look at this Urigwerm," I said.

She gave me my look. Watchcat had thought my night visitor probably had a non-human body; Urigwerm looked like a green and yellow sea serpent with six legs, or more accurately, four legs and two arms. Reptilian, head and all: more like a seagoing dragon than a crocodile, except for the crocodilian jaws and the absence of wings. I guessed his length at fifteen feet, including three feet of neck, and his weight at six or seven hundred pounds. His belly was barrel-like, his tail muscular, with a spade-like fluke at the end. The legs were somewhat longer than a croc's, the toes webbed, the mouth raggedly fanged.

And the face? Somehow intelligent, but lacking utterly in the milk of human kindness. That mother wouldn't even shed crocodile tears.

I'd bet anything I had that that body never evolved in nature—not on this planet, anyway. Maybe in the vat of some laboratory; that's what seemed likeliest to me. And I doubted it was illusion; illusion might fool the eye, but not the sphere.

My intruder had commanded me to come to him. If that was him, we were about to give him his wish. I could feel my long sword at my waist—I insisted on taking it despite Erolanna's wish—and on the other side a dagger, razor-sharp, balanced for throwing.

My mission was to record Urigwerm's imprint and get back instantly. But if it came to self-defense, I'd test that scaly hide. And it would flunk.

It looked highly unlikely that I'd have to. It was a dangerous environment, right enough, but with the time machine . . . Preparing to record Stalin, I'd felt nervous. Just now I felt cool. A good sign, I thought. Erolanna was pretty quiet, though; she was worried about his sorcery. It seemed needless to me. Even if he was awake, he'd have to be damned fast on the trigger. I'd be recording when my feet felt his floor, and she'd snatch me back almost at the same instant.

He was lying on his throne, a large and sumptuous couch that had to be strong to hold his weight, his head raised on its three-foot neck. Two merchants stood at the foot of the low dais, richly robed. I wondered what kind of ambition would dicker with someone like Urigwerm. If they'd seen what I saw later . . .

They were talking, gesturing, but Urigwerm's mouth opened only to grin or laugh. Neither grin nor laugh kindled much mirth in me. His laughter was understandably inhuman, a hollow, grunting, booming sound. He must communicate like Watch-cat, I decided, impinging verbalized thoughts on the mind.

"When is that?" I asked. "Present time?" It was morning at Amodh Veri.

She nodded. "I wanted you to see him in the light. This," she added, "is where he sleeps." The picture changed, showed a chamber with a pool some twenty feet long and half as wide, but shallow.

His bed, I supposed. "I will send you back to last night there," she said.

"Will the recorder record if he's under water?"

"I recorded the imprint of a large goldfish in a fountain yesterday."

"I'll bet that was exciting. What'd it look like?"

"Primitive and dull."

She changed the view again, to the same chamber by night. In a shallow wall niche, a low flame flickered in a lamp, a bowl of oil, making shadows jump like massed specters. But the specters were only the shadow of the crenelated rim of the bowl, enlarged and projected. In the dark pool I could dimly see the bulk of Urigwerm.

I stepped to the rhombus as she put the viewer on the spot where I was to land. Everything felt fine. There was the now familiar instant of suspension. . . .

And I was standing not in Urigwerm's bedroom, but on a sandy beach at the edge of scrubby forest, looking out to sea.

Damn! I thought, *he's got the place burglar-proofed!* Or shielded against magical intrusions, more likely; otherwise ships couldn't get through. Apparently the rod and sphere were more powerful than his magic—they'd come down from Spekthos—so we could look in on him. But his magic was more powerful than Erolanna's time machine, so I'd ended up deposited on the shore.

She was probably looking at his chamber right now, wondering where in hell I'd come through. In a few seconds she'd likely tell the sphere to find me, wherever I was, and snatch me back. She'd said once that if I ever failed to go through where she'd targeted again, she'd do that.

But I didn't *want* to go back yet; I wanted to look around. And if I didn't want to go—didn't intend to—I didn't have to. Because at this end, *my* intention was senior. What I wanted to do was wait around and see where I was. Would the castle be visible somewhere offshore by daylight? Was there a port nearby? What were the possibilities of going to the castle as, say, the bodyguard of some merchant that visited Urigwerm?

Not that I'd do something as crazy as that. It'd be interesting, but it wasn't really vital that we record him, merely desirable. And even accepting Watchcat's belief that he wouldn't remember our earlier confrontation, he'd almost surely pick up that something was strange about me.

And on top of that, it looked like Erolanna wouldn't be able to reach in and snatch me back.

Still, it would be interesting to snoop around here a little—do some research.

A larger wave washed up the sand, and I stepped back from it. *Okay,* I thought, *right or left?* I went right.

What if, for some reason, I had to get back to Amodh Veri on my own? Amodh Veri was in what had been France. The Inner Sea had been the Mediterranean. But where was I on the Mediterranean? Greece? Spain? The moon told me I was on an east-facing coast; that could be a lot of different places. Even Tunisia, or Sicily. I'd play hell walking back from either of them.

The Lord of the Inner Sea. I wondered if his shield covered the entire sea or just part of it. Lucky I hadn't put down in five hundred fathoms of salt water ten miles out.

The moon also told me that dawn wasn't far off. It was in the fourth quarter and well up into the sky.

Ahead of me in the sand were the marks where someone had dragged a boat across the beach and into the woods. An attempt had been made to brush them out, but close up they were apparent. Following them, I found a dinghy about a dozen feet long, concealed behind a thicket well back among the trees. She was built to seat a small mast forward and had a shallow keel, but the mast was gone and so were the oars.

It occurred to me that they might be hidden nearby, so I decided to hang around until daylight. Just in case it turned out I wanted a boat. Crawling beneath another thicket not far away, I told myself to wake up when it was getting light, then went to sleep with the recorder by my side.

The eastern sky was well lighted when I woke up, although the sun hadn't appeared yet. One last star shone clear and bright in the southeast, like Sirius might have. But this looked bigger and brighter than I remembered Sirius, and too near the southern horizon. Maybe there'd been a nova or supernova in our part of the galaxy.

But it held my attention only for seconds, for some three or four miles offshore jutted the abrupt rock topped by Urigwerm's castle.

And my decision was made. I'd become a housebreaker and kidnapper and was prepared to commit murder; I might as well add boat-theft to the list. I found the oars in a nearby hollow log and didn't look for the mast. Tucking the recorder inside my shirt, I put the oars in the boat, dragged it into the water, and climbed in.

Briefly I had trouble with the oars—I was used to oarlocks, and the boat had thole pins instead—but I got the hang of it, and what little wind there was was from the west, so I made good progress. The sun came up. Now and then I looked back over my shoulder, correcting course, and after a while the great rock loomed only a quarter mile ahead.

I stopped rowing to look it over. It jutted some two hundred feet above the sea. Two low wings of rugged rock, volcanic dikes, extended from its base a short distance, sheltering a small anchorage where a pair of single-masted ships lay.

Presumably someone on the walls above, or in a tower, had noticed me by now, but hopefully considered me insignificant. If they didn't—well, I probably wasn't worth a storm, but there were still those "certain creatures that live in its waters" that Erolanna had mentioned. Maybe, I thought, I should have waited till evening and made my approach by dusk. And what in hell was I doing out there anyway?

Play it be ear, I told myself.

So I rowed leisurely into the little anchorage, to one of the small ships there. A burly, hairy character leaned on the rail with his forearms, watching me.

"Ahoy," I called, "how do I get up there?" I gestured skyward with a thumb.

"Ye got to be called and expected. Then they has somebody waitin', and they comes out for ye."

"Waiting where?"

He thumbed back over his shoulder. I couldn't see at what—the ship was in the way. I thanked him and rowed around her, examining the sheer rock face ahead near waterline. There was a small grotto, looking to be fifteen or twenty feet wide at the water's surface, with six or eight feet of clearance. From where I was, a hundred and fifty yards away, I could see a portcullis across it to prevent entry.

I sculled the remaining distance casually, in hopes of avoiding excessive interest. Any interest that drew action would be excessive.

The portcullis grating was much too close to

squeeze myself through. Farmond couldn't have made it. I gripped the bars and peered in. The roughly rounded cavity was artificial—a tunnel, not a cave. Bigger inside than at the mouth, it extended in farther than I could see, with several feeble oil lamps in the first hundred feet or so. There was a loading dock along one side, carved from the rock wall, a yard or so above the water.

Presumably there were stairs somewhere in there that would take me to the castle. If I could get in; the only possibility was that the portcullis did not reach the bottom of the tunnel. I looked up. Because the sheer rock face was stepped back, about eighty feet up, I could not be seen from the castle; I was visible only to any disinterested sailors who might look my way. And to Erolanna, who probably figured I'd gone completely bonkers.

I tied the boat to a ring beside the entrance. Then I made a crude carrying pouch of my shirt, put the recorder in it, and tied it to my belt with the lace from the shirt-front. Avoiding the question of why I was doing any of this, I slipped into the water and dove downward to the bottom of the portcullis.

It ended some thirty inches from the tunnel bottom; I kicked under and then up, surfacing without blowing. Somewhere in there might be a guard I hadn't seen. I stroked to the loading dock and pulled myself from the water.

My eyes had adjusted to the available light, and I could see farther up the tunnel. Near the next to last lamp, a small barge was tied to the dock, and I padded silently to it. Three pairs of oars had driven her, and a steering oar was shipped in the stern. She was painted, though I couldn't tell the color in the dimness, had decorative carvings along her rail, and there were actual cushioned seats for passengers. I decided it must be how guests were brought in from visiting ships.

Beside her, a stairwell opened into the tunnel wall, unguarded, better lit than the tunnel itself. I didn't feel good about using it. It was too narrow for active swordplay, or for any swordplay except thrusting, and attackers could come at me from above. If they had pikes or halberds, that would be end of game for me. Fini!

So I went on to the final lamp. I couldn't believe they carried supplies up those stairs, although in a slave labor situation they might. And by the last lamp was, of all things, an elevator. It was like nothing that ever came from the Otis Elevator Company, but it was an elevator, a box about six feet square and four feet deep, with a front gate that let down on hinges for easy loading. Chains attached to stout five-foot corner posts, joining above to a single heavier chain. Somewhere up above must be a big winch, probably powered by a capstan.

I could have climbed the chain, but by the time I reached the top, my arms and hands would be so tired that I'd be at a serious disadvantage in a fight. And a slender cord hung down from above; I decided it must be a signal cord.

What the hell, let them hoist me. That's what Urigwerm had slaves for. I bellied over the gate and pulled the cord. After five or six seconds, the lift began to rise, and not so slowly as I'd expected. The winch must have a big drum, I decided, with lots of manpower on the capstan.

A little light diffused down the shaft from the top, and I wondered if someone would look over the edge to see what their cargo was. As the light grew stronger and the top nearer, I began to watch upward. It occurred to me that, at any time, they could simply stop winching, and I'd be at the mercy, if any, of whatever bowmen they might call.

Then, above me and some twenty feet or more below the top, I saw another tunnel where it met the shaft. I prepared to abandon ship there on the fly, but to my surprise, the elevator halted. Apparently my single pull on the cord had ordered a stop at that level, and the chain, I decided, must be marked to tell the winchmen where to stop.

I got off. The tunnel was flat, its floor smooth, and a freight cart sat by the shaft. Twenty-five feet farther, it opened into a room. I left my sword in its sheath; a place this size would have a big staff, and I needed to look like one of them going about his legitimate business.

The room was a storeroom, part of the kitchen complex, with wicker baskets of produce and fish. I walked in as if I owned it, and I almost did. There was one other person there, bent over and examining the contents of a basket. He didn't look up. One broad door led through a dozen feet of dark rock into a kitchen. A narrower door led into a curving passage, and I chose it.

That was a mistake. It ended in a wine room, and the wine room had a guard. He stared truculently at me as I entered.

"Has Cadmus been here?" I asked.

He scowled. "What Cadmus? I know no Cadmus."

"Short, fat. No? If he comes here, tell him to report to Charley Judge. At once." I turned sharply and walked out.

So I went through the kitchen after all, and none of the busy workers there gave me more than a glance. The reputation of the castle and its master, its unassailable position and dominating appearance, and finally the portcullis over the only apparent entry, had made internal security lax.

Either that or they knew something I didn't.

There were three ways out of the kitchen besides the way I had entered. I took the nearest, which led into a meat-cutting room unoccupied at the time. I was surprised at it. It sloped to a central drain, and the heavy wooden meat-cutting tables and smooth stone floor were clean-scrubbed. There was a door on the other side, and I tried it. It opened into a meat locker, where smoked carcasses, halves, and quarters hung in rows on hooks—beeves, sheep, hogs, and . . . I closed it quickly, stood there for a few seconds getting myself together, and went back to the kitchen.

This time I took the widest doorway and started up a broad flight of stairs, which at once left the interior of the rock itself for the stone block structure of the castle.

It took me to a service corridor, lit by frequent large lamps supplemented by a window at the left end. At the right end was a short flight of steps with two men-at-arms at the top, guarding a door, their six-foot halberds at parade rest. I stepped back out of sight, untied the makeshift pouch, and took out the recorder. The shirt I left next to the wall like some large dropped rag. Especially with a gymnast's physique, it was better PR to go bare-chested than to wear a shirt heavily wrinkled and soggy with salt water.

Then, with the recorder in one hand, I stepped back into the hall, turned right, and strode down it, doing my Darth Vader impression. As I approached the stairs, the two halberds came down, their owners less concerned with the unlikely possibility that I might be a threat than with the proper ritual.

"Halt!" said one. "Who are you, and what do you here?"

I gave him my best haughty expression. "*I* am Charley Judge," I said, and held the recorder against my belly in both hands. "I have a message to give to the Lord of the Inner Sea, from the Guardian of Ixmatl. I am looking for the throne room."

"This is not the correct entrance," he answered. "This is a service entrance. You must go to the guest entrance."

"And where is that? I have not been here before." I made it sound a trifle testy, as well as haughty, and he decided I might be someone important, regardless of my simple kilt and roman boots.

"Go to the other end of the hall," he said, "then turn right. Go to the end of that hall and turn right again. Continue to the antechamber of the throne room; they will let you know the time of your appointment."

I scowled, nodded curtly to fulfill his expectation, about-faced, and strode off.

The corridor lengths suggested that the throne room might be large, and it occurred to me I hadn't gotten a look at much of it when we spied on Urigwerm—only at the dais area. And I hadn't checked on the guards.

Of course, I hadn't expected ever to be there.

As far as that was concerned, it still wasn't too late to backtrack, climb down the chain and get back to the boat. But instead I walked into the antechamber.

The guards here clearly were not the turkeys the others had seemed. Two big blond halberdmen, who must have been twins, stood by the double-door entrance to the throne room, barbarian mercenaries for sure. Their stony faces bore ritual scars, and other scars that looked fortuitous. Their uniforms were about right for guards of some eleventh century Byzantine emperor. Two other guards stood opposite each other against the side walls. These were blacks, their heavily-muscled torsos bare above broad sashes, wearing only loose pantaloons. Shoeless for footwork, they wore swords in their sashes, nearly as long as my own. They scowled when they saw me; they were no soul brothers.

But my immediate problem was a thin, supercilious, cold-eyed old bastard in a long dark robe. His arms were crossed like a mandarin's, hands concealed in loose sleeves. I walked directly to him and nodded slightly, the recorder held at my waist in both hands.

It occurred to me that he might read minds.

"I am the legate of the Guardian of Ixmatl," I said curtly. "I have brought a message for the Lord of the Inner Sea."

He smiled, a smile I'd hate to expose my back to, and when he spoke, he hissed his esses. "The Guardian of Ixmat? Have I heard of him? What district does he rule? Is that in the swamp of M'Taro?"

"Old man," I said coldly, "another incident of disrespect and you will die at once. I will state my mission again: I am the legate of the Guardian of Ixmatl. I have brought a message for the Lord of the Inner Sea."

His smile stiffened slightly, his black pupils glittering. His words were oily. "Of course. Forgive me. The Guardian of *Ixmatl*. I misunderstood you, my good lord. Yess." He looked pointedly at my plain kilt, gray with moisture, my plain and soggy roman boots, and smirked, extending a scrawny hand. "Give me the message and I will bring the answer back to you."

I left the hand there between us and looked at him with casual deadliness, saying nothing till he withdrew it. "I do not give the guardian's message to lackeys and sycophants. And this message is not written; I have it in my head." I held the recorder slightly higher. "In this receptacle of the guardian's power, I will absorb Lord Urigwerm's reply so that the guardian may receive his thoughts directly.

"Tell him that."

My insult had triggered a flash of hatred behind those eyes. Now he ducked his head and gave a small insane giggle. "Of course, my lord. I will tell Lord Urigwerm of your presence and of the guardian's wish." He half turned, sidling a step, then went not through the doors but behind one of the floor-length velvet hangings that flanked them.

I looked at one of the halberdmen; he couldn't have cared less what had been said. Then I glanced at one of the black swordsmen; his scowl was gone, but his expression was no less hard. I'd been pushing my luck since daylight; I had a long way to go, and I still had to face the serpent himself.

They let me wait long enough, but that was all right. I was good at waiting when I had to be. Finally the doors opened and the old man appeared, smiling, almost obsequious. I didn't like it; he looked pleased.

"Yess, my lord legate, I am happy to tell you that Lord Urigwerm will receive you personally now."

I nodded coldly and passed through. I hadn't expected to retain my sword.

There was much more than I had seen in the sphere. An oval pool, sixty feet long, occupied the center of the room. All four walls were hung with indigo velvet. Two more tall barbarians stood inside the high doors, these two wearing only breech-clouts, plus harness with quiver and long sword. Each held a six-foot longbow backed with horn, strung and ready, and had the muscle to draw it. They'd have been better off with something taking half the strength and time to use. But they were impressive, and undoubtedly deadly.

On each side of Urigwerm, at about fifteen feet, stood two more black swordsmen, heavy-bodied giants, the largest men I'd ever seen. Twins again, close to seven feet tall and built like sumo wrestlers. Beneath the fat there'd be a lot of muscle. Their broad-bladed swords were so long that, with their naked tips on the floor, their hands nonetheless rested on their hilts.

The focus of the room was Urigwerm on his throne couch, immediately flanked by two female dwarves with crossbows. They, at least, hadn't been there for the merchants. Whatever security had been there then had stood at some remove from their master.

The situation looked as dangerous as a ticket to World War III.

All of this I absorbed as I walked in behind the old man half a dozen steps and stopped. He made a deep obeisance toward Urigwerm. I bowed slightly, stiffly, from the waist, at the same time recording; she had it now, whatever happened.

And then I felt his mind touch mine. He *had* been the intruder, I was sure of it, but there was no sign that he remembered me.

[Bring him to me, this legate,] he ordered. [I would indeed know what the guardian has to say to me. And I have an important message to impart to her. Through him. Bring him to me!]

There was an undertone of derision in his thought. The old man's eyes held suppressed glee as he turned to me and gestured, and I followed him down the rich indigo carpet that curved around the pool.

I didn't trust the pool either. The water was
dyed blue, its depths lost in the color. We stopped
about a dozen feet in front of the throne, at the
edge of the eight-inch dais. The old man bowed
deeply again and backed away to one side; I repeated
my own slight bow. I could feel the pool ten feet behind me.

A dragon *can* grin, or that one could, his irregular teeth dangerous in powerful jaws.

[And so, proud legate, what would the Guardian
of Ixmatl say to me?]

I didn't know how much Urigwerm knew, how
much he remembered, what was all right to tell
him. It had to be something that ended with me
being sent out of there alive and well, yet didn't
compromise our position.

"The game of mankind is nearing its final days,"
I said, "and must be won. The guardian is establishing who her allies are. You have seemed an
antagonist till now, but it is not too late to cast
your hand on the side of the guardian and Juokal."

I could feel his amusement. [Juokal? Juokal? He
is a myth. There is no Juokal.] Like a light, then,
he turned the amusement off. [But you did not
come to talk to me of Juokal. Why are you here?]

"I am here as a legate from the Guardian of
Ixmatl. I am here because she sent me. And there
is a Juokal. Not the Juokal of superstition; she
speaks of Spekthos/Juokal, who came down from
heaven in power and knowledge."

[Spekthos/Juokal? Juokal by any name is myth.
I am god enough for man. Tell me more of this
Spekthos/Juokal. I may find it amusing.]

I nodded curtly as before. "A long time ago,
Spekthos came down from heaven to teach man,
and took the form of a man, but he was killed
through treachery, and abandoned us, returning to

heaven. And his memory came to be called Juokal. Now Spekthos is interested once more in the possibility of salvaging man from his debased state. He would save you, too. The guardian will assemble the ablest beings she can, in an effort to convince Spekthos to participate again."

By the time I was done with my little speech, I felt sure that none of this meant anything to him. Perhaps he wasn't Shu-Gwelth after all; perhaps Sbu-Gwelth was waiting in the wings somewhere.

Or this might be Shu-Gwelth, and he might simply not remember. Like everyone else. Three million years is a long time.

A remarkable sound came from the long throat, a resonant purr. He looked at me for perhaps ten long seconds that seemed longer. I waited, saying nothing more, sensing that he was getting ready to speak.

[Legate, why should I ally myself with her? This game you speak of is none of mine. And men, to me, have the sole importance of slaves—knowing slaves or unknowing slaves.]

"Does the name Wlkwos mean anything to you?" I asked. I saw no slightest sign of recognition. "Or the name Shu-Gwelth, which in its time meant Accursed Liar?"

His eyes withdrew introspectively, and after a moment the long head swung slowly from side to side. [Perhaps—perhaps they may have once. But if so, it was long ago, in a time long forgotten.]

He broke the mood then, his attention back on me. [Your guardian is a fool to imagine I would join with her. In only one thing is she correct: The end of the game, if we regard it as a game, is indeed at hand. I myself have already set the final act in motion, and there is nothing she can do to stop it.

[And when it is over—when it is over, *I* will rule the world that follows, as the victor. And the guardian, for her effrontery and for the millennia upon millennia of interference I have suffered from guardians—the guardian will continue, will persist in unending degradation. I have the means! I have not been idle all this time! They say she is beautiful. Is she? You have seen her. I will keep her that way: beautiful. And she will be the whore of whores, on display in the market places for the amusement of the most depraved. Yes! Performing tirelessly like a marionette, but aware! Always aware! I have the means!

[And Spekthos? If there is a Spekthos, he wears flesh. And if he interferes—if he interferes, I will, I will—*have him impaled!* Yes! I will have him impaled!]

He paused then, peering at me insanely.

"Is that the message you want me to take to her?" I asked crisply.

The casual simplicity of the question startled him out of his mania. He stared thoughtfully, and his head began to nod. Slowly he grinned. [You will take nothing to her. I will *send* you to her in a basket. When I am done with you.]

I leaped. Not at him, but at the dwarf on his left, swinging backhand on the draw, felt my sword strike, and leaped again, clearing couch and dragon, striking at the other dwarf as she swung her crossbow toward me. Instantly I turned to Urigwerm, and from the corner of my eye saw something rising from the pool—an ugly head, part of a rubbery body. It didn't slow me, but I was distracted, and my backhand stroke at the rearing Urigwerm missed the neck, grating along the hard bone of his long upper jaw, to glance off the sloping forehead.

A lashing tentacle from the pool reached short. I lunged at the squalling Urigwerm as he rolled off the couch clutching his face, his caterwauling striking me with a force beyond sound. My blade thrust deep through scaly hide, through ribs, through organs as I felt, rather than saw, arrows slicing the air toward me, glimpsed a fat swordsman swinging, and fell sprawling on Erolanna's floor. She burst into tears.

I got to my hands and knees, pressing my palms on the floor until the shaking stopped, then got up. I realized what had happened: My last stroke had killed Urigwerm, who'd died more quickly than I would have expected of a reptile. And with that, the shield was gone. It turned out that Erolanna had kept the viewer on me constantly, and when the action had started—it had lasted less than five seconds—she'd at once begun again to try to pull me out of it.

It had been harder on her than on me; she'd been a helpless bystander until Urigwerm had died. I hugged her and stroked her hair and got blood on her gown, and told her, "Hey, lady, don't cry. You saved my ass!" She hiccuped through her tears, called me some names partly in affection and partly in exasperation for doing what I'd done, and was functional in a minute or two. Then we checked in with the sphere to see what was going on.

The throne room had emptied of all but the bodies. The recorder lay broken where I'd dropped it; not shattered—it was strong stuff—but a curled projection had broken off. I offered to bop back and get it, but she said the power was gone from it now and she could make a new one.

As she picked up the imprint viwer, the thought hit me that perhaps the recorder had not been able to transfer the recording out through the shield. But it had. And there it was: Urigwerm *had* been Shu-Gwelth.

We didn't know who he'd be next, but I'd cost him his base of operations and the influence of his identity.

SEVENTEEN

The next two days were a lot quieter. I got back into my "routine"—working with the troops, riding, reading. I even spent a little time with Watchcat, answering her curiousity about my life before Ixmatl.

But I still got in a couple of micro-time jumps, each taking me back a few seconds to Dhomes Bodai. Erolanna wanted Uno Ulao at Amodh Veri; if he was to be a member of the fellowship, we needed to be able to confer with him, and unlike the emeriti, he had no sphere.

So the day after the excitement, I went back to ask him if he'd move in with us. I told him about Urigwerm and what he'd said about having set the last act in motion. I wasn't surprised when he agreed readily. What did surprise me was that he said he'd be ready the next day. He didn't, of course, have a lot of material goods to bring, but he did have a monastery to turn over to a new master.

But he said everything was so routinized, and the activities so largely unvarying, that it would be both simple and easy.

The next day I went to help him through. He

had only two wicker hampers of belongings. He wasn't even bringing any books, which surprised me, although he did bring the scroll—both in the original language and the translation. He said the books belonged to the monastery.

We moved him into the room next to mine. He loved Watchcat at once, although, to my surprise, she was somewhat reserved toward him. I introduced him to the cook, who was her usual grouchy self.

The guard troop was making good progress. Ranzil was a good drill master when I was gone, with no compulsion to change the drills I'd given them. The men were well over their initial soreness; their flexibility had begun to improve noticeably, and they were considerably less awkward.

I created some little drills for myself to improve my horsemanship—laying out patterns to ride around and assigning Farmond to mark them out with small cairns of stones. He didn't look terribly thrilled with the job—I think it reminded him of the farm. But such is the life of a squire, or my squire, at any rate.

On the third day, her new recorder finished and tested (our signatures came out the same), she contacted the emeriti and called a conference. Besides us, there were the three emeriti and the three trainees. I was the only one that wasn't psychic—a magician of some skill. My single "magic trick" was surviving. And that wasn't really magic, it was training and quick wits. And intention. Well, maybe it was magic of a kind at that.

It was an awkward conference to start with, although it worked out okay. Each sphere could only see one place at a time. Each emeritus kept hers on Erolanna pretty much of the time—on Erolanna, Uno, and me, that is. So they were all watching us, but they could also see our sphere and whoever was on it, while Erolanna switched from one to another of them as they talked. The main problem was that she could only hear the one she had on the sphere, which severely inhibited their ability to volunteer comments.

She introduced Uno and reviewed the scroll with them, the whole thing this time. Then, using her sphere, she showed Bherk-Kari addressing the crowd, and I told them how it had seemed to me, listening there. After that she showed them Uno's signature, and Jikan Kulo's, and finally Wlkwos's. After that we all watched Uno in the ruins of the old monastery, remembering how it had been after the impaling.

When he was done, Erolanna showed them Bherk-Kari's imprint and told them her number one priority was to find who Spekthos was in present time. Meanwhile, she would explore the possibility of contacting the game recorder at a time prior to the Rod of Knowledge, although that seemed an outside chance. The idea was to find the time/place vicinity of the original game agreement.

Then she told us there was a third approach to winning the game, one which did not depend on anyone other than ourselves or on any equipment. She wanted the emeriti and Uno to begin creating the points of an agreement which might lead godlike beings into a mess like the present and longtime state of man. The idea took me totally by surprise; I'd never have thought of that.

I got the floor and told them what I thought my role ought to be. Shu-Gwelth/Urigwerm had said he'd already set the last act in motion. I believed it would be military. And I wanted the job of fighting and frustrating any action, military or otherwise, aimed at closing us down before the others could solve the basic problem. In other words, I considered my job to be buying the others time.

After the conference I felt depressed. It's so damned easy to say what should be done and what you're going to do. But what we were up against looked to me, just then, damned near impossible.

I told Erolanna that.

"Charley Judge," she answered, "you are right. But please look at the things you have done recently, beginning with that night in the snow when you departed your friends. Then tell me about the nearly impossible."

EIGHTEEN

Anyway, I didn't have time to indulge a depression; I had a game to play. One I was unwilling to lose. "So what's the biggest military power on Ixmatl?" I asked.

Uno looked on interestedly. Outside of Dhomes Bodai, he knew little more about present-time Ixmatl than I did.

"Gilgaz Koth has the largest and most powerful army," Erolanna replied. "No other ruler can assemble a force large enough to threaten more than an immediately adjacent territory, nor control an area a quarter as large as his empire. But the empire is a thousand miles from here—a thousand miles, several great mountain ranges, and a hundred kingdoms. He would have to draw his forces from all his conquered territories to undertake a campaign that could reach us here, and he would quickly be beset with a score of revolts. It would destroy him."

While she was telling me this, we went over to the sphere and she got a view on it. I saw a city by a large sea, with a large palace nearby, backed by a narrow coastal plain. Behind the plain lay ancient mountains, deforested and worn. It would

have looked about right in the more backward
Middle Eastern provinces of 1987; all it lacked
were a few Bentleys, Rolls Royces, and Cadillacs.

"That is the city of Gilgaz Koth," she went on.
The view changed to show only the palace and its
immediate surroundings. "And that is his palace."

"Just a minute. Give me a closer look at the
harbor."

There were maybe a hundred small ships docked
there or at anchor. "Is that normal?" I asked. "That
many ships?"

"I do not know," she answered. "I do not know
what number is usual."

"Well," I said, "all the docks are filled, and there
are maybe fifty more riding the hook. If it was
usual to have anywhere near that many, they'd
have more docks. If they have docking for fifty
ships, I wouldn't expect more than maybe thirty
there at any one time."

She wasn't one for needless guessing; she changed
the picture. "This is one year ago," she said. I
counted. There were about twenty tied up and
none at anchor.

"Let's look around the compound outside the
palace grounds," I said. She got the palace again,
in present time, showing an area of small adobe
buildings close by. "Can you find an armory?" I
asked.

Quickly she got one, an open-air operation shaded
by reed awnings. Several men were busy at small
anvils, rapping out arrowheads with hammers, tem-
pering them and dropping them into baskets. As
we watched, one man picked up his basket, and
we followed him to a nearby area where other
men were fitting the wicked-looking heads onto
shafts already notched and fletched. Interesting, I
thought. They weren't crossbow bolts and were

too short for longbows. They'd seem to be for cavalry then.

Next we found a shop making swords, short swords, the blades only about eighteen inches long. Probably to avoid breakage in battle.

She let the sphere wink out, and we looked at each other. "So Gilgaz Koth is readying for war," she said, "and you believe the ships signify that they will travel by sea to attack us here." She examined the idea. "An invasion by sea has not been carried out in modern time. Surely they will need more ships than that?"

"They're pretty small, all right, but they'd probably hold a hundred or a hundred and twenty infantry each, plus supplies for the trip. I'll be surprised, though, if they don't take along a lot of cavalry. Let's take a closer look at the ships."

A lot of carpentry was going on. In every ship we examined, they were building tight stalls for horses below deck and gear lockers above. Apparently the troops would be quartered on deck. Crazy, I thought. They could lose a lot overboard if they hit really heavy weather.

A hundred ships. Hardly enough for cavalry. Erolanna gave me an aerial view again for an actual count, and the number was one hundred and fourteen, including a little flotilla of seven that sailed around the point while I was counting. Call it one hundred going on two hundred.

"That's it, sure as hell," I said. "They're coming here—in force. It's just a matter of time. Late this summer, if they get it together fast enough. Otherwise, next summer; I can't imagine they'll risk winter storms with troops on deck and horses on board. Horses are notoriously poor sailors."

The sphere winked out, and Erolanna stood there

staring thoughtfully through it. Finally she turned
to us. "Charley Judge, Uno Ulao," she said, "I need
to be alone."

I wouldn't have been surprised if she'd had a job
for me next morning, but she sent no word, so I
followed my "normal" schedule. On horseback I
had Farmond work with me with wooden practice
swords. We practiced attack while chasing, defense while fleeing, and face-to-face combat. I did
better than I'd expected. Not that I beat Farmond
up; the main purpose was to keep my seat and
control the horse while in action.

The troops were getting the feel of sophisticated
techniques and their new, longer swords. It made
them cocky. I was careful to encourage that; cocky
was how I wanted them. They'd get better faster
that way, as long as discipline was maintained
and we kept demanding improvement.

I ate with the men, and at supper, Uno came
around and waited for me. We walked together to
Erolanna's. He'd changed since our little session
in the ruins—seemed stronger, more certain.

"I used the time diagram last night," he told
me. "Actually last night and this morning."

"Is that right?" I felt a little pang when he said
it, and realized it was a feeling of loss, as if I was
being displaced to some degree. *Well I'll be a son-of-
a-bitch*, I thought. *Jealous!* "Where'd you go?" I
asked.

"To the city of Gilgaz Koth. The guardian needed
a spy—someone who does not appear formidable
and is telepathic."

"What'd you learn?"

"That the situation is indeed dangerous. She
will tell you."

I'd known it was dangerous; that had seemed obvious. But I hadn't been nervous about it. That's just the way it was. Now, hearing it from Uno, I felt my guts tighten a bit. Why was that? Because Uno felt that way and he was telepathic? Was it *his* emotion I felt that tightened my gut? As I looked at it, it passed.

"You are partly right," he said. He'd been reading me. "It *was* my fear you felt. But not because *I* am a telepath. Rather because, to a degree, *you* are. Many people are." He slowed so we'd have more time to talk. "Emotions have more force than thoughts; they are more easily discerned. Many people feel the emotions of others. A few like yourself sometimes recognize when an emotion is not their own, when it is someone else's. That is the first step in the direction of functional telepathy.

"Others develop a large degree of psychic deafness, even against emotions."

"Hnh! Any chance I might learn to read thoughts as I go along? Aside from thoughts of someone like Erolanna and Watchcat?"

"It is possible. But very few do, even of those who are sensitive to emotions. Even of those who strive for it. Most become less sensitive after early childhood."

He gave me a small, wry smile. "If I could consistently, or even usually, bring persons to a level of enlightenment sufficient to include telepathy, I am sure the monastery would have overflowed with novices."

We walked into her study; she was waiting for us. "Charley Judge," she said, "I have work for you."

My attention was still on what Uno had said— that if a person got enlightened enough, he'd become telepathic. So—what the hell *was* enlightenment? Would we know it if we had it? Maybe it would turn out to be the rules of the game. Maybe we'd never know. I jerked my attention to Ero-lanna's statement.

"Work for me? What is it?"

"I want you to kill Gilgaz Koth."

It took a minute for my chin to stop bouncing off my chest. "What—is that all about?"

"Last night, after we viewed his preparations for war, I visited the emperor's mind. Let me explain. Telepathy does not—cannot—operate *through* the sphere. But the sphere permits me to focus on the mind of a distant person much more effectively. Without it, especially without any strong pre-existing affinity for the person, telepathic contact at a distance is very difficult and uncertain.

"Viewing that person in the sphere, contact becomes much easier."

"I got it. What did you learn?"

"I learned that my suggestions, my ideas, no longer touch Gilgaz Koth. He is too strongly dominated mentally by someone else."

"Urigwerm?"

"Almost certainly."

"He's dead now."

"Seemingly; death is a very transient state. And in the case of a being as powerful as Shu-Gwelth, even having no body might not wholly incapacitate him."

"Okay," I said. "So you want me to kill Gilgaz Koth. That's quite a policy reversal."

"Yes. Are you reluctant?"

"No, just surprised."

She nodded. "Of course. But this is a critical time. If he lands even a few thousand mounted soldiers on our coast, the army of Gel-Leneth cannot stop him. And if I must flee, and operate from some undedicated site . . . As we have found repeatedly in the past, guardians who must move from place to place are seriously impaired. Even when a new site has been found and dedicated as our own, it is years before it serves"—she looked around her—"as well as this one does.

"And if we are entering the final stage of the game, we must not lose our effective base of operation.

"The emeriti agree.

"Gilgaz Koth has decided on invasion over the objections of his advisors. They feel that for him to leave and take an important part of the army will endanger the security of the provinces by inviting revolt.

"So if you kill him, there will be no invasion. In fact, there may well be conflict between those who would wish to succeed him.

"And if, from this assassination, my powers should weaken, then Adana, the last previous guardian, is ready to take my place until a trainee is fully prepared. You can use the time diagram, or Uno can, to bring them quickly."

"All right," I said, "so what's the plan? Transfer into his bedroom and use the sword instead of the recorder?"

"Yes."

I'd have expected her to seem really heavy, having made a decision to assassinate someone, but she was totally matter-of-fact about it.

"When?" I asked.

"It should already be dark there. I will look in on him after a while. When he is asleep, I will send for you."

"Okay," I said, and started to leave. Something was bothering me, but I hadn't looked at it yet.

"Charley Judge," she said as I walked toward the door, "tell me about it."

I stopped and turned to her. "I just wish you hadn't told me this far in advance. Basically, I just discovered I'm not an assassin at heart. It's not going to be all that great, waiting to go murder someone."

Her face went sober on me. "I am sorry, Charley Judge. I did not realize."

"Of course not. I didn't either." Old blood and guts, who chops down three thugs and scares two others into helplessness—who sneaks this way into the castle of the Lord of the Inner Sea and chops up a dragon and two female bodyguards. But this was different.

"Sweetheart," I said, then stopped, embarrassed, for Uno was standing there with us—"it's no big deal. I'll go find Watchcat; I haven't visited with her for a couple of days now."

Watchcat and I strolled and sat in the dusk and in the fragrance of the night, and I realized I had as much affinity for her as for Erolanna. But different. Our communication was on a finer wavelength, deeper and more subtle. After a visit with Watchcat, I always came away feeling wiser and more . . . spiritual.

It turned out that existence through a long sequence of lives had been no news to her. The mind travel back in time, that she'd mentioned earlier, had been the revisiting of past lives. And she had not always been a leopard. In fact, this was her first life wearing spots, so far as she had found.

"Did you know me before?" I asked. "In some earlier life?"

[Not that I know of, Charley Judge. But it is

quite possible. I have visited relatively few of the many.]

"How do you do it? How do you decide what lives to look in on?"

[I decided what I wanted to understand about myself. On the principle that the key to understanding my present conditions lies in experiences in the past. But I have stopped doing it, as I told you. I need to find a safe procedure. It is not, I believe, that it is unsafe to look back. But what I need to look at, for my purposes—what I need to look at is dangerous to revisit. I believe now that I encountered one of the penalties which guard the secrecy of the agreement, as told of in the scroll.]

"Huh! What was it like?"

[It was as if I was suddenly wrapped around by something I could not see. And then I knew nothing. I became unconscious, beset by feverish dreams that were afterwards forgotten.]

She got to her feet and gave a stretch that was actually more of a feline squirm. [I do not wish to talk more about it now. It is as if talking about it makes the darkness draw near.]

I shivered. It seemed to me that I could feel it, too. So we talked about worlds she had visited, and other lands on this one. But the darkness stayed with me.

It was close to midnight when Erolanna sent a girl after me. About two AM at Gilgaz Koth's palace. Uno had already gone to bed.

The emperor had finished romping with his girls of the night and sent them back to harem. We could hear him snoring. I went to the rhombus, the sword in my hand honed to ultimate fineness.

I looked at Erolanna, and briefly she looked at me, her eyes a mystery in the pale light of the

crystal glow lamp. I didn't feel like Charley Judge—
Sergeant Charley Judge, reputed super-warrior. I
felt—what was it I felt? Melancholy was part of it.
But mostly it was fear, a low-intensity fear. I nodded at her and she turned to the sphere. I took a
deep breath. . . .

And I was there, in the strange darkness. A sea
breeze moved the curtains. Gilgaz Koth lay on his
back in a white nightgown, mouth slack. One arm
was out to the side, and I got a strange notion of
him strewing flower petals. The quiet snoring was
not in his throat, but back in his nose, as if he had
adenoids.

Carefully I positioned myself by his head, an
appropriate distance to one side, and gripped my
daito with both hands. I shifted my feet, as if they
needed to be just right, then adjusted my hands on
the grip. They felt clammy. The night, the room,
the situation seemed unreal. It was as if I was
outside myself, watching, in a dream where everything is in slow motion. As if the air I moved in
was a viscous fluid. The place was pregnant with
expectancy. Slowly I raised the sword. *Get it over
with*, I thought. It paused overhead.

Then *swuck!* The blade struck downward, its
quickness taking me by surprise, cleaving the neck,
cutting deeply into the featherbed he lay on, and
his body gave one great spasm.

The stroke alone had been fast, and I stood
waiting, waiting for Erolanna to snatch me back,
to find myself standing in the rhombus again. The
feeling of strange expectancy, of unreality, was
gone. There was only the darkness, the soundless-
ness, the breeze moving the curtain. I shivered
with reaction.

Nothing happened, and still nothing. After a minute or two, or maybe only twenty or thirty seconds, I began to realize she wasn't going to pick me up.

Shu-Gwelth. It was the only explanation I could think of. After I'd come through, he'd slapped a shield on. It didn't make sense; how could he have known? But I was sure of it. And the sense of expectancy—whose expectancy had it been?

Briefly waves of chills ran over me, and after cleaning my sword thoroughly on the bedding, I padded to the door. I could hear nothing there, but there were almost certainly guards on the other side. So I went to the window—French doors, actually—and peered between the curtains. They opened onto a balcony.

No one was there—I hadn't expected there to be—and I walked out to peer over the balustrade. A garden lay some twenty-five feet below, large and walled. There was no moon to see by, only starlight. Something moved in the darkness and emerged into an open space, a huge dog, Dane-size. I could assume there were others.

I went to one side of the balcony and examined the wall for climbing. Part of my ninja training, such as it was, had been wall-scaling. I'd never felt comfortable with it. The stone blocks here were about eighteen inches high and two feet long, and the mortaring was not flush. There was space enough for fingers and toes, in places an inch deep.

The risks were obvious. I might fall off. Or a dog might see me and make an uproar, although dogs don't look up much. And there was still the door as an option. But how many men, and how much potential uproar, on the other side of it?

I tied my roman boots to my belt in back, shifted my scabbard behind my left hip, and climbed onto the stone balustrade. Reaching to the side overhead,

I found a crack with my right fingers. Next I reached out with my right foot, and then my left hand. So far, so good. Very, very gingerly I raised my left foot from the railing, supporting myself by fingers and toes. There was a brief feeling of paralytic numbness, and I clung there, knowing it would pass.

Slowly then, one hand at a time, one foot, feeling for the deeper spaces, I crawled up the cliff of the wall. It went better than I'd expected; I'd make it as long as not a thing went wrong.

I bypassed a window to my left, resisting the temptation to try my luck there, deciding to go for the roof. I thought how neat it would be if I climbed up through the shield and got whisked back to Amodh Veri.

But some twenty-five feet up I came to the end of the climb—a little ledge where the wall was set back about six inches. Above it the blocks were smaller, the gaps too narrow and not as deep. Ten or twelve feet farther, I could see the parapet of the roof, unattainable.

Spread-eagled, I moved to my right, like some overgrown spider, sliding my sweating forearms along the ledge. After twenty or thirty feet the ledge became the floor of a sort of small balcony, but set into the side of the building. There was room between the balusters for my hands, and in seconds I was over the railing.

The balcony was about ten feet wide and six deep, and held nothing but a small square planter at one end, with a leafy young tree raising its head above the balustrade. In the back wall was a narrow wooden door with a bolt handle sticking through the slot. For some disgusting reason it wouldn't open. The hinges were on my side, so it would open outward. I tried to visualize what might be holding the bolt; it might be possible to jimmy it.

Give a look, Erolanna, I thought, *and tell me.* But there was no response. Apparently the shield was proof against telepathy, too.

I looked along the wall in both directions. It extended to the distant corners of the building, unbroken at this height by window or other balcony.

Maybe, I thought, I'd have to climb back down and try a lower window after all. I looked down the wall and felt weak. It was an axiom that going down was a lot harder than climbing up. I seriously doubted I could make it.

So I sat down behind the balustrade to rest and wait for inspiration. If I did have to climb down, I'd just have to do it without falling off. My fingers brushed along the floor. And it was clean! There was no noticeable accumulation of dust or grit; it could have been swept in the last day or two.

What the hell was this balcony? It occurred to me that it might have a function, be used by someone for something. At any rate, somebody watered that tree. Maybe the door would open, come morning.

That was all the encouragement I needed to keep from trying the downward climb. I lay down where the door would bump and waken me if it opened. After a bit I slept.

NINETEEN

Daylight woke me. Actually, the hard floor woke me, several times, and when I saw it was daylight, I decided to call it a night and stir around. I stretched like a cat and raised my head above the balustrade to see what I could see.

I was looking westward toward the sea. Some two hundred and fifty or three hundred yards to the northwest and southwest were other palatial buildings, though much less imposing than this one, with their own walled grounds, their upper walls brightened by the rising sun behind me. I saw movement on the side of one, on a little inset balcony below the roof. A tiny figure stood with both arms raised, as if greeting or praying to the rising sun. After a minute or so the figure disappeared.

I looked at the other building, and there was a similar balcony there. As I looked, a figure emerged onto it, too, to stand with arms raised.

I didn't notice how long he stood there; I was distracted by a sudden wild yammering down below, and realized that someone had just found Gilgaz Koth.

So what next? Pretty damn soon, someone in

authority would arrive and start looking around, asking himself questions. If he was sharp, he might look up. Chances are they'd check the room behind the window I'd passed by, to see if someone had dropped a rope and entered that way. But the odds were that they wouldn't think of the balcony, which was well off to the side.

Meanwhile, what I needed was someone to unlock the door behind me. Maybe for prayers. The ones I'd seen seemed to be greeting the newly risen sun, but this balcony faced west. So I'd have to hope they prayed to the setting sun, too.

It promised to be a long, dry, hungry day.

Later in the morning I heard the voices of men talking and arguing in the garden below. Needless to say, I didn't look over the balustrade. Not once did I hear anything through the door. Mostly I sat on the floor where I'd be behind the door if it opened—*when* it opened. And off and on I dozed.

Finally the sun lay swollen and red on the rim of the sea in the northwest. If it was going to happen, it would be now.

It was. I heard a rattle at the door, stood up quietly, saw and heard the bolt handle slide. The door opened.

He didn't close it behind him but stepped directly to the balustrade. His robe was golden yellow, and he wore a peculiar hood-like cap that came loosely to the neck in back. Putting both hands on the railing, he lowered his face, as if preparing himself, then raised his arms high and began a quiet rhythmic chant in some dialect, probably archaic, that I caught only a little of.

I didn't touch him until he stepped back. Then I gripped him hard at the base of the neck and pinched out his lights. His robe fitted well enough; it didn't reach my feet as it had his, but two or three inches didn't seem like any big deal. The cap was fine too. The smart thing to do, I thought, would be to kill him—choke him or hold the carotid artery closed until he died. What I settled for was to raise him with both hands and bang his head hard against the stone wall. Not hard enough to kill him, but he wouldn't be yelling "help" for a while.

Beneath the robe was a cotton tunic, gathered at the waist by a knotted cord. I pulled it off, too. For insurance I took the four-foot cord, tied his hands high behind his back, and looped the other end around his throat. Then I cut a long strip from his tunic, used it to tie his ankles up behind him, and connected them with his wrists. He'd find that to struggle was to choke. With part of what was left of the tunic, I gagged him. When he finally woke up, he'd have a tiger of a headache and be pretty uncomfortable in other respects.

I didn't know what to expect as I followed the narrow corridor and long, narrow stairwell. Except for the robe and cap, I didn't look even remotely like the guy I'd mugged. If he was the only one around here that wore an outfit like this, then I'd have been better off to wear the tunic. But at least the robe covered my sword.

I found my way down more halls and stairs, passing some people along the way. I caught some glances, probably because of my color, but no one seemed startled or perturbed. The final stairs led to a tall, broad hallway, where I glimpsed another yellow robe entering a door and out of sight. So far, so good, and I could assume this was the ground floor. I strode importantly along to where the hall entered a sort of rotunda. There was the wide main entrance—and a squad of soldiers guarding it. Four of them held crossbows.

I turned toward it, never breaking stride. How far was it, I wondered, to the edge of the shield? Fifty yards? Three blocks? Three miles? The officer in charge stepped to intercept me.

"Your Reverence," he said, "no one is allowed to leave the palace."

"I know," I said. "I am taking an urgent message to the admiral."

"The admiral?"

"Of course," I said impatiently.

His expression didn't change, but his eyes looked worried.

"Quickly! It's urgent!" I changed my tone from imperative to confidential. "Man, the security and stability of the Empire are involved. Come now! I'll be back within the hour. And I'll see to it that your loyalty and good judgment are properly recognized and rewarded."

He wasn't buying it. "Your Reverence," he said apologetically, "I have my orders from the chancellor, no less. Personally. It grieves me, but I must deny you while I send to him for approval. I'm sure that as a priest, you'll be delayed only very briefly. I'll send to him at once."

Without taking his eyes off me, he spoke to one of his men, and the guardsman left on a dead run. The officer was doing a damned fine job in an awkward situation.

I decided my best chance was to wait, hope that the chancellor or someone of comparable magnitude showed up, and maybe I could grab him as a hostage. The guardsmen weren't overtly threatening, but they kept their eyes on me, ready. It occurred to me that I might get away by just stalk-

ing huffily back the way I'd come, but somewhere
I'd still have to confront a guard squad to get out.

So I stood, grumbling. It was taking longer than
I'd expected, and I didn't like the feel of that. Then
someone who might have been the chancellor himself arrived, with an old man in a robe like mine;
they stopped ten feet off. The old man stared hard-
eyed, shook his head curtly and said one word—
"Imposter"—then turned and walked away.

The chancellor's square, hard-mouthed face
looked my death warrant at me. "Take him to the
dungeon," he said, and followed the old man as I
felt a crossbow against my back.

The guardsmen still seemed respectful enough
as they walked me to the dungeon. I suppose it
was the robe. But there was no doubt they'd kill
me if I tried anything. At the dungeon, the keeper
relieved me of my robe: "We can't have *this*
in chains," he said. "It'd be irreverent; if you
please . . ." Then he saw my weapons and blew a
silent whistle through rounded lips. They all backed
off a step, then the guardsmen closed on me and
took them.

I looked at the guard officer. "Captain," I said—I
was probably promoting him—"on the balcony
where we pray the setting sun to return, lies a
man bound and gagged, and no doubt unconscious.
Send someone there to free him." Then I turned to
the dungeon keeper. "I have had neither food nor
drink today. When you have tethered me, as I
suppose you cannot avoid, have supper sent. The
new emperor will want me undamaged and well
cared for. Now, shall we go?"

The man who bolted my leg iron on was careful
not to make it needlessly tight. Not thirty minutes
later a fairly passable stew was brought to me,
with an actual spoon! Apparently the dungeon staff

were willing to assume I was someone of importance who might later be freed to remember any offense. And no one had given them any contrary instructions.

It may or may not have occurred to the chancellor and the old priest that I might be the assassin. But they were no doubt busy on the more important question of the succession: Who would be the new emperor? That could be vital to their futures—possibly even their lives. When that was settled, someone would probably see to my "examination." I'd better be out of there by then. Meanwhile, where there was life, something good could still happen. Theoretically.

I was in a cell about twenty feet across, with chains around the walls for twelve, but there were only two of us. I asked my cellmate about that, and he looked at me as if I was an idiot.

"Didn't you watch the executions last week?" he asked, and that's all I ever heard him say my whole three and a half days there. He was apparently a hard case, and probably jealous. He was chained hand and foot, while I wore only a leg iron. And later that evening a jailer came dragging a bag stuffed with straw, leaving it by me for a bed, while my roomy had only the hard, cold stone. Also, I got three more or less decent meals the next day; he "ate" once, apparently a gruel, for he drank it from a clay bowl.

Well, I thought, *some has it and some don't. You can always cheer when they take me to the axman or the torturer. If you're still here.*

The day after that, they brought in a new prisoner, Santho. He was lucky, too: only a leg iron.

"What's happening out there?" I asked.

He barked a short laugh. "Who knows? Koth's

idiot brother, Gorthog, has stopped drooling and talked. Actually! He actually spoke! It astonished everyone. Not just a few idiot words either, though that would have been surprising enough. He talked like everyone else. I can't see how it was possible: One learns to speak gradually, with practice. Everyone's talking about it. He must have been bright all those years, only feigning idiocy. Maybe he thought it was safer that way.

"Though if I'd been Koth, I'd have done away with him as an unsightly nuisance. You've seen him, I suppose?" Santho wagged his head amusedly. "Koth actually seemed fond of the little toad. Now the toad wants to be emperor, and a week ago there were those whose job it was to change his diaper for him."

He chuckled. "And his cousins, who'd already started for each other's throats, have their heads together now like camels at a spring. They're all out to get rid of Gorthog, because he's in the direct line of succession while they are not. When they've gotten rid of him, they'll return to knifing one another. It could be weeks before there's an emperor again."

He seemed to remember where he was then, because he stopped talking and sat back to brood. I wanted to hear more. There had to be somehow some way that I could weasel out of the hole I was in, but I needed information.

"You don't think Gorthog's got a chance then?"

He looked back at me and then thoughtfully at the question. "Oh, a chance, I suppose. Old Terzuk's obviously protecting him; otherwise, his cousins would have him dead by now. And Terzuk has other generals behind him. But Gorthog's only a bargaining point; he'll trade him away to whoever will give him the most authority. Whoever will give him the army.

"None of the cousins have the strength that Koth had—his guts or his brains. If I could get my hands on the assassin. . . . A dozen years from now, or less, the empire will look like the jackals have been at it: pieces from Dhunkar to Thantim to Vork lost to barbarians. And business will be ruined."

The glitter went out of his eyes, and he slumped back. "Not that it'll make much difference to me. I'll be lucky to be alive, and my property will be gone."

When supper came, I whispered to the guard that I had a confidential message for the dungeon keeper. He looked suspiciously at me but nodded. Half an hour later he returned with manacles and a key, handcuffed me, and unlocked my chain from its ring on the wall. Together we went to the dungeon keeper's office. Two other guards were there, playing a card game, but they stopped when we came in, and watched me.

"I have made a decision," I said, "on whom to give my support. I want to send a message to Terzuk."

He stared at me.

"Give me paper and pen," I ordered.

It was there on his table, with an ink pot. Reluctantly he got up and gave me his chair. When I'd finished, I blew on the ink to dry it, then read it over to myself.

Dear Terzuk,
    I am known in the west as the world's greatest fighting man and military tactician. I have techniques of armed and unarmed combat

which are unknown to any other. You are well known as a man who appreciates excellence— both effectiveness and distinction. I came to your land because only here can my abilities be properly appreciated and made use of.

I would like to demonstrate my skills to you. If allowed to use my own familiar sword, I will fight at one time any three champions you are willing to waste, and kill all three promptly.

> Charley Judge
> Warrior of Ancient Earth

It looked okay to me, as long as his champions weren't too damned good. I'd forgotten to mention my humility, but this ought to at least pique his curiosity.

The dungeon keeper looked it over and was impressed enough that he told the guard to leave my manacles on when he chained me in the cell.

The third day came and went with no further change. It was on the fourth that they led me, still handcuffed, out of the dungeon. The guards that took me turned me over to another squad of guards, whose breastplates and helmets were polished bronze, worked with silver. The officer with them wore a breastplate that appeared to be silver worked with gold, and his helmet was plumed. A very royal-looking bunch.

I decided there must be a new emperor after all, and if there was one so soon, it had to be Gilgaz Gorthog, the only contender on the direct line of succession. The idiot brother. I was afraid I knew the explanation for his remarkable recovery.

The throne room demonstrated again that aesthetics was not dead on Ixmatl, just poorly distributed. But the figure on the throne was not aesthetic. Short and misshapen, it had an ugly hairless head with bulging eyes. Shu-Gwelth—I was sure that's who it was—had looked much more aesthetic wearing the green and yellow of Urigwerm's scaley hide. He'd looked like a lord of the sea should look.

"You know me!" said Gorthog, and crowed with pleasure. "How delightful!" He gestured for my escort to leave. They about-faced sharply and marched out, leaving me in my chains and Gorthog protected by four bodyguards.

"We have privacy now," he said pleasantly, gesturing at them. "These are deaf mutes; my brother, too, liked confidentiality. You know, I was afraid for a time that we'd lost you, and I wanted to thank you for making me emperor here."

"Yeah," I said. "Win some, lose some."

"M-m-m-m. A philosopher as well as a great warrior. Indeed! Despite the burdens of establishing and securing my authority here, I have given time to the question of how I might reward you for, m-m, your good services."

He laughed again. While he was in such a playful, talkative mood . . . "One reward," I said, "might be to clear up a mystery I have. How did you know to put a shield over the palace, a shield against magic, so I couldn't escape after I killed Gilgaz Koth?"

"Ah! First, when you ended my existence as Urigwerm that day not long ago, you immediately disappeared. I did not realize the significance of that at once. It is a great shock and loss to be murdered in the prime of one's power. Yes. Especially violently and in terror. A great shock. But even bereft of my body as I was, confused and stricken, I realized that with my death, you had disappeared at once.

"Afterward, recovering, I understood what had happened. The guardian's power was much greater than I had imagined. Much more dangerous. She had removed you by her magic. Because of my weakened condition, my shield against the sorcery of others had ceased to be.

"Then, in my good brother's chamber, I was visiting his mind when you arrived. I say my good brother because I had already preempted this ludicrous but most opportune flesh. Its previous, ah, occupant was, poor thing, unable to prevent me.

"So I was visiting good Koth's mind, whispering my good advice, you see, and suddenly became aware of an intrusion. I knew you at once, and what your purpose was, and it occurred to me that it would be to my benefit that you succeed. Indeed, I could not have prevented you. At that moment I put a shield up, for I did not want you to leave before I could thank you properly.

"Then I almost lost you again, for I was still closely connected with his mind when you struck. I had not known how great a shock that would be to me. I snapped back at once into this." He tapped his head. "After I had recovered myself, some uncertain time later, I could not find you, and thought I must have lost the shield momentarily in the shock of my brother's death. And then, of course, I was quickly beset with the most urgent matters of the succession."

He actually sighed. "The powers of even a god, I fear, are not without bounds, lest there be no contest to enjoy and no pleasure in existing. Nor are the lives of a god without their pains and loss.

"But you will soon know more about pain and loss."

He looked at me for maybe ten silent seconds, his large eyes hooded by swollen, half-closed lids. "I thought to exercise some interesting techniques on you in public display. It seemed appropriate. But alas, this crude people has limited views of what constitutes acceptable behavior, and an emperor should not offend his people needlessly. Especially when his position is newly secured and his power not fully accepted.

"The important thing is to deprive you of that dangerous and excellent weapon you wear, that body. Torture would be but a pleasant embellishment, which I will deny myself. In the name of political wisdom, you will die in the tradition of my beloved people, in the manner of a regicide.

"Astonishing as it may seen, the army actually felt affection for Gilgaz Koth. Yet they will be as interested in seeing *how* you die as in *that* you die."

He turned to a bodyguard, gestured, and pointed at the entrance. The man bowed and trotted from the room. A moment later my escorts came in and removed me.

I wasn't returned to the dungeon. They simply kept me under close guard in a nearby room for what must have been two or three hours. Then I was marched out to what seemed a drill field, a depression some hundred yards across, surrounded on three sides by slopes covered with soldiers. The air buzzed with their voices. In the center of the field a gallows stood—a single stout post with a well-braced arm jutting out eight feet on both sides. I wondered how long it would take to choke to death. A lot less time than it would take to die over a slow fire.

The buzz increased as I was marched across the bare dirt, then lessened as we reached the post. What I read as the dominant emotion was not cruelty, though that was there, too, and strongly. The dominant emotion was interest.

And the gallows had no rope. Instead, from a pulley on each end hung a slim, strong chain with a wrist iron.

"Are you right-handed or left?" asked the officer in charge. I looked into his stony eyes for a clue to what the question meant for me, and learned nothing.

"Right-handed," I said.

One of the guards crowded my left manacle as far up my forearm as it would go and put a dangling wrist iron on my wrist. Another bolted it snugly. Then they removed the manacles, took the slack from the chain, and hoisted me three feet off the ground.

The buzz of the crowd increased.

A man stepped up from the rear of the detail, carrying my long sword. The officer took it from him and, at safe arm's length, extended the hilt toward me. With my free hand I took it.

I was beginning to understand.

Several mounted men had entered the field and began now to circle at a canter. The crowd sound increased further. I would not be able to fight or talk my way out of this one. The best I could do, I thought, would be to go out with style.

A trumpet blew, and the rider most nearly in front of me turned toward me, spurring his horse to a gallop as he drew back his sword. Dangling like a fish, I waited, my own sword poised, and at the last moment he swerved, whooping, not striking. There was laughter and minor hissing from the crowd.

The circling horsemen continued their canter. Another trumpet blew; another rider peeled off and charged. He did not swerve; I knew he wouldn't. As he galloped by, I met his sword with mine, and it was his that spun away into the dirt while I spun and jerked from the impact. The crowd cheered loudly.

It wasn't particularly hot, but I wiped sweat from my eyes with my forearm. No trumpet sounded as I swung on my chain, but when the motion stopped, it pealed again, and another rider charged. Like the others, he would pass on my sword-arm side; there was a code of honor at work here. We swung, blades clashed, his broke, and mine, though deflected, struck him from his horse. As I jerked and spun, I heard the crowd roar, saw the horseman tumble in the dirt, sprawl, then scramble to his feet, one arm clutching the bloody other as he trotted hobbling from the field.

The crowd sound faded as the trumpeter raised his horn. He blew. Again one rider charged, and again swords shocked together, and this time both blades broke. There was an "Ah" from the crowd, not of pleasure, but like the release of pressure. Then there was silence from the mass of watching warriors as I swung and twisted slowly on my chain.

So this, I thought, *is it.*

When my motion stopped, the fifth trumpet blew, but no warrior peeled from the circle. Instead, one stopped with a cloud of dust, turned toward me and reared his horse, its front hooves pawing the air. It was a salute, the execution a ritual, and I the brave bull. And because I had fought well, I would die quickly, not be hacked and mutilated before a jeering crowd.

When the hooves struck the earth again, he

spurred his horse into its charge. The world slowed, and each stride of the war horse was a powerful, inexorable lunge. My senses were so finely tuned that, as he neared, I could feel the thud of hooves carried upward from the ground through the gallows post, saw the rider's grimace of concentration, lips flecked with spittle, eyes bulging. The action slowed even further—the sword in its terrible swing, sinews taut in the arm, fine wires beneath the skin. I stared, the roar I heard my own . . . and landed heavily on all fours in Erolanna's garden! I'd done it again without the time machine! Slack-mouthed, I rose to my knees, shaking all over.

And howled. "Watchcat!" I bellowed it. *"Watch-cat!"* Then collapsed on my face in the grass.

TWENTY

When help came, though, I refused it, shuffling to my room, where I holed up like a sick grizzly. A couple of times, early on, Farmond asked if there was something he could do. After that he kept a low profile, bringing my meals and scurrying out again. Even Watchcat, who'd kept a vigil outside my door to begin with, had left.

That's how heavy it was around me—not fit for man or beast. I felt like I hated everyone. I didn't, really, and knew I didn't, but that's what was going on with me. I was being a hundred and ninety pounds of pure ugly. I didn't even shave or bathe, though I hadn't washed since I'd left to kill Gilgaz Koth.

Erolanna had looked in on me once, minutes after I'd gotten back—stepped into my room and I glared her back out without a word. Uno didn't show at all; he was probably moving out next door. If it was bad for Farmond being around me, it must have been a lot worse for telepaths.

Charley Judge, I thought to myself, *you are a miserable turkey mother. Either get it together or get your black ass out of here. They've got enough problems without you making the place uninhabitable.*

So I got off my bed and strode grimly out into the hall, headed for the stable, to ride until I straightened out. Maybe I'd head west and explore those timbered mountains.

But there was Erolanna in the hall, coming toward me. As I steamed ahead, she stopped, as if to speak. I focused my eyes past her and locked my jaw, not slowing.

"Charley Judge . . ." she began.

I said nothing, passing her like some kind of stone man, like a tank—like some robot operating on a circuit, not responding to its surroundings.

"Charley Judge," she repeated after me, "I need your help."

I turned on her. "That's bullshit! Stop playing on my sympathies."

I glared at her calm and quiet beauty. She hadn't said it beseechingly—the "poor helpless me" flow that some women use. She'd simply asked for help, as if there was a pickle jar she couldn't get the lid off of.

"It's too heavy for Uno Ulao and me," she said matter-of-factly.

I stood there feeling my hostility deflate, even though I knew I was being had. "Okay. What's too heavy?"

"A statue I wish moved in the garden. Come, I'll show you." She was turning as she finished, and started down the hall again.

"God damn it, Erolanna, wait a minute!" I said, a stride behind. "I don't like to walk behind someone!"

It was going to be like my mother and her migratory furniture; it was never in the right place for her. I'd moved mom's living room suite, especially, many times. That's one reason I was such a strong kid: My father was away a lot, I was the only boy, and mom liked her furniture solid and heavy.

Uno saw us coming and brightened right up. *Who do you think you're kidding?* I thought at him. The statue was a slender marble elf or fairy, with pointed ears, and curls that would never need a comb. Remarkable that that image hadn't changed.

"I can take one end and you the other," Uno suggested.

"Not unless you want it in two pieces," I grumped. "Marble breaks." I looked around. "Where do you want it?"

"Right over there," Erolanna said with certainty. I'd heard that before, too.

I showed Uno what I wanted him to do, and we took it there. She stood back, looked, and nodded approvingly. She didn't even change her mind and have us shift it around a couple of times.

"Do you have time for tea?" she asked.

"I might as well," I said. "A quick one." We walked back in, and Uno excused himself to go elsewhere. No doubt about it, they'd set me up.

"Look," I said as we sat down in her study, "you took advantage of me." I was going to add that the statue had been just an excuse to . . . what?

"Assassinations were originally your idea," she said. "In this instance, I felt it was appropriate. It seems I was wrong."

"That's not what I was talking about, and you know it! I was talking about the statue. You just used it to get me to talk to you."

She smiled slightly. "You are right. I did think, several days ago, that I would like it moved. But today I took advantage of it. And of you. Was it all right to do that?"

"Huh! I've got to admit I feel better. Matter of fact, a lot better. I guess it was what I needed."

Her smile got larger. "Charley Judge, one of the things I like most about you is that you are a remarkably honest person."

"Good," I said, "because I've got more to be honest about. I've just spotted what's been bugging me, or part of it, anyway. You want to hear it?"

Serious now, she nodded.

"Do you know what I found in the city of Gilgaz Koth? Besides, almost, my death?"

"No. What?"

"I found some basically decent people. A little nuts, maybe, but decent. I found honor. I found a culture that doesn't tolerate the rack. I found loyalty—misplaced, maybe, but loyalty. I even found people who still have some drive.

"So what the hell am I doing, having them for enemies? I don't want to kill those people!"

"Fine. Then do not have them as your enemies. Be their friend."

I looked sharply at her. She was going to trick me again.

"I mean it, Charley Judge! Be their friend!"

"But they're planning to attack us!" I said. "Conquer us. Drive us out or kill us, or make us slaves!" And there I was; she'd done it again. I'd been turned around one hundred and eighty degrees without even a ring in my nose. "What are you getting at?" I demanded.

"Let us see if I recall the words, the final words of the scroll," she said to me. " 'And from that forgathering will come the end of the game of Weirro/Ixmatl. Whether it ends successfully, with the players set free, or simply grinds to a stop, leaving mankind mired and lost forever.' Something like that. Do you believe the scroll was accurate in this?"

I nodded. I recalled the people I'd seen in the time of Bherk-Kari and the sense of energy and optimism I'd felt there. The reason people were so down now was that they'd been defeated so repeatedly in a game that was rigged against them. Rigged to lose. The people in the empire showed there still could be a resurgence. But Shu-Gwelth would use them and then stamp it out of them. Urigwerm had said as much, that day in his castle.

"I see your point: It would be no favor to let them win. But hell, I never figured to. What was going on with me, I guess, was, I was feeling sorry for myself. I really don't like to kill people. And here I am in charge of one-half of a goddamned war. Or a pending war, anyway."

"I know," she said, "And regarding killing, it is interesting that, by having you kill Gilgaz Koth in the name of peace, I put Shu-Gwelth in a position of greater power, not less. No, killing is not the key to life. Knowledge is. But we must not sacrifice ourselves and thereby accomplish the lingering living death of all. It is necessary that we win the game.

"Life is precious to its owner. And Shu-Gwelth, when he spoke to you as Gorthog, made it clear that a man can be harmed—can be lessened in his life to come—by the nature and circumstances of his death. Perhaps that is one of the secrets of the accord.

"But if his life is precious, he will nonetheless exchange it someday for another. So his life is less important than his future."

It felt like something I'd known since I'd first read the scroll. I just hadn't looked at it, seen what followed from it. "You're right," I told her, "but try telling man that. He knows his present life is real."

I got up. "I was going to go riding," I said. "Want to go with me?"

"Not now. Tonight."

"You've got a date, lady. If I can take a blanket along."

Like I said, she's learning to grin.

TWENTY-ONE

Two days later I left again, but this trip was different. On horseback to Gel-Hoveth, capital of Gel-Leneth, it was my first conventional travel on Ixmatl of any length at all. Farmond and I rode all one day over a rolling countryside of pastures and occasional districts of crop land, with forests in the narrower valleys.

On the second day we crawled from our blankets with the first bird songs and were in the saddle before sunup. The country became rougher—forested, except on the broad, exposed ridge tops where sheep grazed, their bleating and bells never still, audible for miles; we were never away from the sound.

In midafternoon we took a break on an open crest, enjoying the sun. After that I walked a bit, less to rest Wind than because I was saddle sore. The "road"—a saddle trail much shorter than the coach road—dropped into a leafy tunnel. In minutes I could hear the next stream below. I wondered how far we were from Gel-Hoveth; I'd been told we could make it in three days. By pushing and by eating cold rations, we'd see if we couldn't do it in two.

It was about then we ran into trouble—six armed men mounted on nondescript plugs. They were as surprised to see us as we were them. Two had crossbows, and all carried short swords. One raised his crossbow and snapped off a shot at me from about one hundred feet, missing, taking Wind in the brisket. I'd let go the reins before the bolt struck, dodged into the trees as I heard Wind scream, and charged. I heard the ugly snap of the other crossbow but neither saw nor heard the bolt.

They'd have to dismount to crank up their bows again, if they were like the other crossbows I'd seen in Ixmatl. A stupid weapon for a horseman.

They totally stopped, confused at one man charging them on foot, and the hindmost four half turned, moving off the trail. The one in the lead kicked his horse into a trot, entering among the trees, sword raised to cut me down. He was right-handed, so as he closed, I dodged to his left, wheeling around a young tree, and took his foot off above the ankle, the follow-through hacking the horse on the ribs. It reared; the rider screamed and hit the ground heavily.

One of the others came at me then, tried to turn broadside to block me while he struck. These turkeys were dumb, and poor horsemen to boot. With his short sword, he had to lean to strike. I parried his off-balance stroke to my right and rotated my blade, taking him in the arm. It didn't have a lot of force, but it was razor sharp; he, too, screamed and fell off, and I jumped on his barebacked horse, on my belly, grabbing at the mane and trying to get a leg over as the animal wheeled. But I accidentally cut it in mounting, and it lunged forward while I was still only half aboard, dumping me off its rump. One of the crossbowmen had dismounted to crank up, and the horse that had dumped me ran over him as I charged at the next nearest horseman.

At that moment Farmond struck. His daito was smaller than mine but outreached their short swords, and apprentice though he was, he had more skill and poise than they. He closed with one, yelling a wordless war cry, parried the man's crude chop and took him across the chest. The other two turned and fled downhill as his opponent flopped heavily to the ground.

"Catch me a horse!" I shouted. Farmond snapped out of his battle trance, looked around, and trotted to the mount of the trampled bowman.

The man whose arm I'd cut sat white-faced on the ground, staring at me as I walked toward him. He wasn't even trying to stop the flow of blood from his arm.

"Grab it!" I ordered. "Pinch it together with your hand or you'll bleed to death." Suddenly aware, he obeyed with a jerk.

Then I went to the man I'd struck first. He was still alive, though unconscious, but even as I bent over him, the blood flow from his stump slacked as his heart stopped.

The man the horse had trampled lay on the trail with a broken leg and probably other injuries. He was in shock, gray-faced, mouth working in apparent defiance; he figured I was going to chop him.

"You'll live," I told him. Then I went to Farmond's adversary. The kid was stronger than he looked, at least in blood lust; his stroke had severed ribs and breastbone, driving into lungs and heart. This had been the other crossbowman. I took the weapon, cranked it, and loaded it with one of the bolts the man carried.

The guy with the arm-cut sat still white-faced and staring, but holding his wound tightly now, blood trickling through his fingers. I pulled the tunic off the dead bandit, sliced it into bandage, and snugged it over the guy's wound.

"My squire and I are headed for Gel-Hoveth," I said. "We'll let someone know you're here. If you want to wait around, maybe they'll send someone. And maybe they'll help you or maybe they'll hang you."

After that I looked at Wind. He was on his side, his eyes open but dull, his breath rattling with the blood in his lungs. I told him he was a good horse, then cut his throat.

Finally, on an impulse, I went to each dead man, laid his body out full length, folded his hands over his chest and closed the eyes. If the recent occupants were hanging around in grief, they could use a little respect. Farmond, trailing a horse behind him by its rawhide reins, watched curiously from his mare. "Makes their spirits feel better," I explained.

"Yes, sire," he replied. I wondered what he thought. Swinging down from the saddle, he offered me his own horse, a proper courtesy from a squire to his tutor. We transferred saddles and other gear, Farmond picked up the other crossbow, and we mounted to leave.

The bushwhacker with the crippled arm called to me. "Your lordship! Would you leave me for the wild dogs? They'll smell the others tomorrow for sure and come running."

"Then you'd better have your swords to hand," I told him, "so you can defend yourselves. Or maybe your two pals that ran away will come back and help you."

His pale eyes stabbed hatred at me as we rode away. "Would you leave *me* for the wild dogs?" he'd asked. Not *us*; mentally he'd abandoned his crippled buddy, even in his request for help. Well, I sure as hell didn't owe him anything, and I wouldn't willingly go around carrying a rattlesnake in a gunnysack, to quote my Georgia daddy.

Again we went to bed with the birds and got up with them, and were on the trail before sunup. The country had smoothed out and gotten more civilized, and after a couple of hours we hit the coach road. I spent some saddle time thinking about what I'd tell King Thelmar. I wouldn't mention Gorthog's strong interest in the guardian; she could end up a bargaining piece, if Thelmar was inclined to rabbit.

On the coach road we encountered a patrol; I told them about the attack and the wounded we'd left. They weren't very interested, and I doubt they sent men out. Too far out in the boonies maybe; anyone who traveled there did so at his own risk. And sheep country with a lot of timber would attract brigands, because they could steal sheep as needed, to live on.

The nag Farmond was riding was making better time than I thought it would, and before noon we could see the city lying in the late-morning sunshine, in a valley on broad Bregh-Sreumedh, the "Great River." Gel-Hoveth was a lot bigger than the town of Blue River—I'd guess it would have twenty or thirty thousand people, maybe more— and it looked fairly prosperous.

Several large villas could be seen on hills near the town, each surrounded by a defendable wall, but Gel-Hoveth itself was not walled, and the countryside looked peaceful. The palace of King Thelmar was a walled compound on a slight elevation below the city, with a large round keep as a stronghold. So far the city had not been allowed to encroach closely on it.

In the valley bottom I was impressed to find the road paved with big slabs of flat rock, squared and fitted, set into a roadbed of crushed stone. Some of the wagons and carts we passed were painted or had painted wheels. This was the big time. Close up, Gel-Hoveth was a mercantile town of late medieval aspect, smelling of minor industries I couldn't identify. The street we passed through on was wide enough for wagons to pass and still leave adequate room at the sides for pedestrians. Outside the palace, we paused long enough for me to don the thigh-length cape Erolanna had provided, white, with the gold stitching that symbolized the House of the Guardian.

We were well received by the household staff, who tried not to stare: they'd apparently never seen a black before. Neither, I suspect, had Thelmar. I showed him, as I'd shown his steward, my letter of introduction from Erolanna. As he read it, I noticed his young attendant, a bright-looking kid maybe fourteen or fifteen years old, who maintained a correct, incurious posture, but whose eyes were interested.

Thelmar frowned when he came to the meat of the short letter, then reread aloud: "... a subject of utmost importance to the security of the kingdom." He looked up at me. "What is this about? We have no enemies on our borders nor rebellion within them."

"What about your western border?"

He frowned again. "We have no western border. To the west is the ocean."

"Exactly," I said, "the ocean. There is someone who is hungry for the fair land of Gel-Leneth. He intends to invade you by sea and is gathering a great fleet of ships to bring his army here. From the city of Gilgaz Koth."

"Gilgaz Koth?" His first response was consternation, followed by disbelief. "The Butcher of Asia? Why does . . . Gilgaz Koth already possesses a vast domain, and there are many lands to conquer far closer than we. And Gel-Leneth is no large kingdom. How are we of such interest to Gilgaz Koth?"

"Geography," I replied. "Gel-Hoveth is a doorway, and the river a corridor. Bregh-Sreumedh is a waterway into the heart and guts of Europe. As such, it is as attractive to a ship-borne invader as it is to the merchants that have made Gel-Hoveth a major commercial city. Thus the conquest of Gel-Leneth is his first objective. It will provide access and a base of operations and supplies for the subjugation of Europe."

The king was wilting beneath the logic of my thesis.

"Gilgaz Koth himself planned it," I went on, "with the help of Urigwerm, Lord of the Inner Sea. Koth is dead now, but his brother, Gorthog, has become emperor, and he continues the preparations."

"And how do you—how does the guardian know these things?" asked Thelmar.

"The guardian has her means. There is little the guardian cannot know when she gives her attention to it."

I was surprised at how shaken Thelmar had become. Far from being a wimp, he was a shrewd, forceful, and intelligent man. In twenty-three years as king, he had secured his borders, resolved old disputes with his neighbors, and substantially improved administration of the kingdom. With a little unknown help from the guardian, of course, but he was strong and astute, and saner than most.

"And Koth is dead, you say. Is Gorthog as dangerous? Koth was a great military leader."

"Gorthog has not proven himself as a general, but he has competent generals, and he is even more implacable than Koth in his intentions."

He sat staring at nothing for a few seconds before looking up at me. "Does Gorthog have the loyalty of those generals? How did Koth die?"

I saw what he was thinking: If Gorthog had murdered Koth and the generals suspected, or even if he hadn't and they thought he had, they might revolt.

"Gorthog didn't kill Koth," I told him. "I did."

"You?"

"Yes."

"I did not know the guardian used such methods!"

"Perhaps once in ten thousand years does a guardian turn to assassination, when a situation is extreme. It is dangerous to the powers of a guardian to use them in violence. But when she discovered Koth's plans, she also saw that most of those around him were reluctant at the venture. They feared for the security of the empire's eastern reaches. Thus there was a probability that, should Koth die, there would be no invasion, and she regarded the safety of Europe as worth the risk to herself.

"Unfortunately, in the scramble for supremacy, Gorthog won, and quickly secured his authority."

"And Urigwerm," said Thelmar. "You said he helped Koth plan the invasion. What part does he play in this now?"

"None. Urigwerm is dead, too."

"Dead? Urigwerm? I do not believe it! He has lived from the beginning of the age, and they say

that, by his sorcery, he does not sicken or grow
old."

"He is dead," I repeated. "I killed him, before I
killed Gilgaz Koth."

"*How?*" he challenged. "How did you kill Urigwerm?"

"The guardian sent me to see him, with no violence intended. And in his arrogance, he tried to
have me killed. Instead, I killed him." Our eyes
met. "Milord," I said, "you doubt my word. And
that is hardly surprising. But let me demonstrate.
Are you holding any criminals for execution? Desperate men of violence, competent with the sword?"

His gray eyes studied me. He nodded.

"Are they in good health? Not weakened by hun-
ger or abuse?"

He frowned at that. "I do not treat my prisoners
cruelly. When one has been condemned to death,
he is held in decent detention until the next execution day. Then . . ." He shrugged and made a chopping motion with his hand.

"Very good," I said. "First I must tell you that I
am more than a warrior. The guardian called me
to Ixmatl from another world, for certain skills
and knowledge that I have. Such is her power; she
is the greatest guardian yet. But it is my ability as
a fighting man that I would prove to you now, for
it is in doubt here. So let me execute those violent
men for you in open combat, with swords in their
hands."

I read his face; he was not happy.

"Your majesty," I went on, "do I seem to be a
monster? The guardian would not have a monster
in her employ. What I suggest is a demonstration
of my competency, which you doubted. If you hold
men awaiting execution, I would shorten their un-
happy wait while establishing my credentials. And

they will die in the relative dignity of armed combat, not kneeling at the block."

His face was thoughtful now, his eyes probing, attentive. "How many could you fight?" he asked.

"How many do you have? I would prefer not more than three at once, if they are trained soldiers, or four if mere hoodlums. I do not like to endanger my life needlessly."

It had been a heavy audience for him. He began to chuckle then, big body shaking, the chuckles rapidly escalating until he rocked back and forth, tears flowing, his laughter seeming all out of proportion to what I had said. After a minute he subsided to giddy chuckling again. "Three at a time if they are trained fighting men. Heh heh heh! Four if mere ruffians. Hee hee hee! You prefer not to endanger your life needlessly. *Haw haw haw!*" He broke into unrestrained laughter again, then calming, shook his head, twinkling at me through wet eyes. "No, no, my friend, blood will not be necessary. I accept the offer as demonstration enough. Yes."

He got to his feet and reached out a hand to me. A strong, firm hand; I suspected he'd practiced quite a bit with the sword in his youth. Then he sat again.

"But surely she did not send you just to tell me bad news. She could have done that by dispatch."

"Your Majesty is most perceptive. The guardian has assigned me to foil Gorthog's invasion. I would like to sit down with you, learn more about your military and naval resources, and talk about strategies."

"Of course," he said, "but first I have three more audiences scheduled, which I must honor." He turned to his attendant. "Karn, tell the steward to provide the guardian's emissary and his squire with suitable quarters." He nodded to me then in dismissal. "And Charley Judge, I will send for you in two hours."

Thelmar's marshal, Ingoth Klar, and a scribe were part of our next meeting. Klar started out pretty reserved toward me, but warmed up after deciding I was for real. My having read a lot in the history of warfare stood me in good stead. We agreed on a broad plan. They would develop the details for their part of it. Meanwhile, Thelmar would not notify his troops and vassals, or other kingdoms, until we knew whether the invasion fleet would sail this summer or the next.

That evening, in our room, there was a knock. I sent Farmond to the door; it was the king's young attendant.

"Sire, may I have a few minutes of your time?"

"Sure. What can I do for you?"

"My name is Karn, sire, and I am the king's second son. I was very interested in your audience with my father—in the things you told him. Then, later, your squire told me of two times he saw you attacked by greater numbers and that you destroyed them. He said further that you are training the guardian's household troops in ways previously unknown. Then he showed me what he has already learned in only a few weeks.

"Sire, with your approval, I will ask my father if I can apply to apprentice with the guardian's guard."

He looked at me earnestly.

"That's fine with me," I said. "You have my approval. Just what did Farmond tell you?" I glanced at my squire, who reddened just a bit.

"He told how you were attacked by five armed ruffians in an inn, men paid to kill you. And how you killed three before the first body struck the floor. How a fourth fell in a faint while the fifth soiled himself and wept, and begged to be spared. And how, on your trip here, you were attacked by ten brigands, one shooting your horse from under you with a crossbow, and how you rushed them on foot, dodging crossbow bolts, killing three despite their being mounted, while the others fled in terror."

I grinned. Farmond hadn't exaggerated as much as I thought he might have.

"And that afterwards," he continued, "you straightened the bodies of the dead, folded their hands and closed their eyes, to ease the grieving of their spirits."

I put on a more serious expression. "Of course," I said. "And did Farmond tell you the part he played in that skirmish?"

"No, sire."

"He charged into one of them who was in danger of killing me. A mean-looking thug of a man. He parried the man's stroke and sank his sword through ribs and breastbone. The scoundrel was dead before he hit the ground."

The prince looked at Farmond, who was blushing in earnest now. "No, sire," said Karn, "he did not tell me. Oh sire! Now I wish more earnestly than ever to learn from you."

"Karn, as I said, you have my approval and my sponsorship with the guardian, if your father agrees to it. But should he not, let me point out that there are other choices besides that of fighting man. I would not discourage you, or degrade the profession of the soldier, for I am one, and I am proud of it. I only want to point out that there are alternatives of great worth and honor. The guardian is the most valuable person on Ixmatl, and I doubt that she has ever touched a sword. And after her, the most valuable is almost surely a holy man from Dhomes Bodai, named Uno Ulao, who may possibly have touched a sword but surely is not trained to use one.

"My skill at arms has been very valuable to them. But more important is the knowledge I brought with me from my own world. Knowledge, whether of weapons or of other things, is the key. Knowledge of the kind that can be translated into effective use.

"The essential thing is to become skilled in whatever you choose.

"Whatever you decide, Karn, and whatever your father decides, you will be a man valuable to this world. And whatever that decision may be, our paths will cross again.

"Now I wish to rest."

He nodded, thanked us, and left. After a bit, Farmond blew the lamp out.

And I felt Erolanna's thought.

[Charley Judge, I heard you talk to the young prince. You are a warrior of uncanny ability, and you are much more as well.]

[Thank you, good friend,] I thought back at her.

[And was it true that you were attacked on your trip?]

[You bet. Yesterday afternoon. You ought to give it a look in the sphere. There were only six of them instead of ten, but it was a wild minute or two. And Farmond did himself proud.

[And I rediscovered something. It wasn't hard to kill out there, in those circumstances. It was necessary, if I'm to be available for what's yet to come. And I didn't even get mad; I actually felt a little sorry for the dead, even after what they'd tried to do to us.

[You know, there's been a lot of change in me since I came to Ixmatl. In—what's it been? Less than three weeks. You and Watchcat have had a lot to do with it, but Uno's scroll has been the key.

[So when you see him, tell him I said he's a hell of a man. Okay?]

[I do not need to tell him, Charley Judge,] she answered. [He has been beside me these last few minutes, watching you and listening to your thoughts.

[We are a team, the three of us,] she went on. [Without you, we would have little chance. Each of us has been vital, and will be.

[Now we will leave you to your sleep. Come back safe to us.]

When she was gone, I looked at the situation. On the face of it, we didn't seem to have a whole hell of a lot of chance *with* me. But we *were* a team, and we always seemed to pull off what we needed to when the chips were down.

TWENTY—TWO

It was night again, and raining, and we had not made camp. I'd said to Farmond that I'd rather ride in it than try to sleep in it. At least it wasn't pouring anymore, and if it didn't break—well, by riding all night we'd be home for breakfast. We were passing a tiny hamlet that lay a quarter mile back from the road, its cluster of huts and sheds humped dim and dark beneath the storm. Mastiff-like guard dogs roared at us from the perimeter to keep our distance. Lightnings flickered in the east, marking the storm front that had soaked us at twilight, too far away now for its thunders to be heard.

[Charley Judge!]

[Erolanna!] I knew it was trouble. [What's happening?]

[The watchcat is terribly ill. I want to bring you home right now. You are her best friend—her confidant. I do not know what you or anyone can do, but I feel you should be here.]

I turned. Farmond was dozing, his caped figure slumped in the saddle, head bobbing with the horse's gait.

"Farmond!" I said, and his head jerked up. "I

am needed in Amodh Veri at once. I want you to bring my horse in for me."

He stared blankly from within his sodden hood, totally confused.

I clarified, more or less. "The guardian will take me there by magic, and I need you to take my horse home."

His mouth fell open.

"What will happen," I went on, "is that I will disappear here and be there. But a horse is too big for the magic, so he'll have to walk home. You'll lead him. Any questions?"

"No, sire." He looked as if he thought he must still be sleeping.

"Good." I got off my horse, a gelding given me by Thelmar, removed the saddlebags, and handed the reins to Farmond. Then I stepped back away from him.

"All right, Erolanna," I said, "I'm ready."

And there I stood in the rhombus, dripping on her floor, our eyes meeting for just an instant. She left the sphere and we joined Uno, kneeling beside the pallet where Watchcat, wet and limp, lay on her side unconscious. Her flanks moved in and out with shallow breathing, and there was foam on her lips.

"The male watchcat saw her having convulsions in the garden," Uno said. "When it was safe—when she stopped convulsing—two of the servants helped me carry her in."

I put my hand on her head. *Hot!* "She's traveling back in time," I said.

Erolanna looked questioningly at me; I hadn't defined what I meant. "But she is here," she said.

"Watchcat can travel *mentally* in time, leaving her body here. It's something she's done before, and stopped doing after she got sick a couple of times. Now she's done it again. Worse, apparently.

"As hot as she is now, she could die on us, or suffer brain damage." I straightened. "Send me back to before she did it. I'll tell her what's happened—tell her not to."

Erolanna shook her head. "Not yet then, Charley Judge. Let us wait, give her a chance to recover."

"Suppose she dies?"

"If she dies, *then* I will send you back to forestall her. But if she has gone back in time despite earlier dangers, then she must have had a reason."

She got up, went quickly to the recorder and aimed it at Watchcat, then picked up the imprint viewer. "Let us see what this tells us about her condition."

What grabbed my attention at once was the cloud—it was broad and thick and ugly. But Erolanna looked past that.

"The signature!" she whispered.

Small but bright, it was the signature of Spekthos! The halo was a narrow zone, the cloud most of the imprint, but the signature was unmistakable.

And somehow I knew she needed help, wherever she was. I closed my eyes and shouted mentally with my mind, a shout with all the intention I could muster: [Hang on, Diana, the cavalry's on its way!]

When I woke up, I knew significant time had passed, but not how much. It was night, but whether still night or night again, I wasn't sure. I could no longer hear it raining, and Erolanna was sleeping on a pallet nearby. I was seeing through only one eye. I must have fallen and banged my face on something, for the other eye was swollen painfully shut.

[Good evening, Charley Judge.]

It was Watchcat. Diana. Spekthos! I turned over; she was still on her pallet. Uno was asleep on another near her.

"You're all right!" I said.

[Yes, thank you. Although my body is weak and sore. It will soon recover.]

I got a sense of mental chuckling from her and an impression of power and certainty.

"What happened?" I asked.

Uno was sitting up now, and I was aware that Erolanna had entered the room behind me.

[It was as you thought; I left the body and went back in time. To a very critical moment.] Her eyes were calm and steady. [A very dangerous time and place—the presentation and proposal of the agreement for the game of Weirro/Ch'matal.

[Immediately I was beset by pain and fear and desperation—surrounded, as it were, by dense and dirty cloud. I knew these all were subjective, not physical, but they felt terribly dangerous. As in fact they are. Through the discomfort I strove to see, looked thoroughly at what little was visible to me, and gradually could see more.

[I will not tell you what I came to perceive or what I experienced and did. You would almost surely die—at least you would go insane—for the terms of the accord are most powerfully, terribly safeguarded. But after a bit I knew who I had been, why I was able to do what I was doing without myself becoming insane, and why I had not entered the game via the agreement.

[For I am Spekthos, as you know.

[And when I had realized these things, I saw a great many things clearly, one after another in a chain of knowing.]

She had our attention totally, but when she

paused, I became acutely aware of the room. Its silence was a crystal purity in which sounded the perfect drip of water outside, falling onto stone flags from leaves overhead.

"Saw what?" I asked. "What did you see."

The eyes which met mine were amused. [That which you each will have to find for yourself or not at all. And you will. Each of us must learn much for ourselves before we finish, if we are to win.

[Now, Charley Judge, who proposed the agreement?]

"I don't know. Me?"

She smiled, and shook her head like a human might. [Erolanna, who was it that proposed the agreement?]

She answered at once, with certainty. "Shu-Gwelth."

The room was bright with the sense of Diana's delight and mental laughter. [Beautiful, my dear. Yes, it was Shu-Gwelth. And as quickly as I realized that, he shot back through time and attacked me. He was mad with pain and rage and fear, and cast many things at me from an even deeper past, for this has not been our first game as adversaries, nor our most violent. Only the most dangerous.

[And these might have overwhelmed me and destroyed what power I can muster, except for you, Charley Judge. You arrived in fury, with such force, even in your blindness, that Shu-Gwelth withdrew to his body in shock and confusion.

[And then we returned here, you and I.]

She got up and stretched stiffly, wincing.

[My friends, we have much to do. And rapidly, for the game can easily be lost, despite what I have learned. There is little more I can tell you now; I need to think—to sort and evaluate new knowledge. And I must do that alone, for it is deadly yet for any other. Jikan Kulo looked at only the shadowed fringe of it, and died miserably.

[So rest now. We shall counsel tomorrow.]

TWENTY—THREE

With Diana's cryptic remarks, we dispersed to our various quarters. I had one of the servants run hot water for a bath, more to relax in than for cleaning. I was feeling a little depressed, maybe a hangover from my experience with Diana and Shu-Gwelth, although I couldn't remember any of it.

Funny how I'd always thought of Diana as Watchcat, even after I'd named her Diana. "Watchcat" had a certain special feel to it. But tonight that had changed; all of a sudden it didn't seem all right to call her Watchcat anymore. It didn't seem respectful, although the name Watchcat did have class.

And she was Spekthos! My good buddy was Spekthos, whom men had called God, who'd come down full of power and good intentions three million years before and gotten savagely brutalized. And obviously Bherk-Kari's disciples hadn't advanced far enough that they could carry out the project successfully. I wondered if the knowledge she was digging into was as dangerous as she thought. It probably was, I decided; she'd damned near cashed herself in getting into it.

The servant came in and told me my bath was

ready. I walked barefoot to the bath chamber, dropped my robe and stepped in, my breath hissing at the heat, gingerly sat down and felt the tension drain away. Poor Farmond was out there riding through the chilly, soggy night. I'd instruct the servant to see that a hot bath was ready for him when he finished breakfast, which might be a bit late. If the cook gave him a bad time, I'd ask Erolanna to tie the can to her tail and run her out of Amodh Veri. We didn't need someone around who had a case of chronic distemper.

After my bath I went straight to bed, and if I dreamed, I didn't remember it when I woke up.

It didn't take Diana long to do her "sorting and evaluating." She had automatically taken command of the project, with no apparent unwillingness on Erolanna's part, and called an afternoon conference with the emeriti. The conference didn't take a lot of time. Erolanna told them who Diana was, showing them the imprints of Diana and Bherk-Kari. Then, telepathically, Diana gave them a run-down of what had happened the evening before.

After that she told us what the action plan was. As Spekthos, she had known the crystal technology—had passed the basics of it down to the first guardian. With her coaching, Erolanna would now design and construct a new instrument—a time probe. Anyone trained in its use could travel mentally back in time, into their own past—eventually, as they grew stronger, back to their own personal entry into the agreement. When the instrument was tested and its use piloted by Erolanna and Uno, a probe would be made for each emeritus and trainee. They'd be coached in its use.

Each of them would independently have to learn the articles of agreement. It wasn't enough for one person to know. Many would have to. How many, she had no idea. And it wasn't feasible for Diana to learn them all and just make it known. The information was booby-trapped. She was probably the only one who could confront it as she had, cold-turkey, and survive. And she hadn't looked at all of it, by quite a lot, nor did she plan to look again without a probe.

I looked around at the others: none of them showed any skepticism or reluctance. Presumably, as telepaths they could evaluate Diana pretty well.

When the council was over, I was feeling a little—well, like a second cousin twice removed. Not actually an outsider, but not one of the inner group. I wasn't the guardian or an emeritus or a trainee, or even a functional telepath like Uno.

Diana knew what was going on with me. She turned from the now blank sphere and asked, [Charley Judge, who do you suppose was the guardian in the time of Bherk-Kari?]

"I have no idea," I answered. "Is it important?"

[It was the same person who performed the remarkable feat of jumping ahead three million years, taking his body with him, having prepared himself as the supreme warrior in a time when that was possible.]

"You mean I was once a guardian?"

[Exactly. You were then the guardian, and Erolanna and each of the present emeriti and trainees were my—Bherk-Kari's—students.]

"Hey, wait a minute!" I glanced at Erolanna. "Then she and I aren't the same person in two different incarnations?"

[Correct.]

"Then what about the similarities of our signatures?"

[I do not know. But it is an enigma of little

importance. Perhaps you will find out for yourself someday.]

I looked at that. "Well, if I'm not also Erolanna in this time, I must be someone else. I mean, if a person doesn't really stop existing but just goes from lifetime to lifetime, I must have come up the line like everyone else. I must be someone today, or some *thing*, besides Charley Judge."

She smiled, looking at me, really seeing me. [You are Charley Judge today; no one else. What were the years of Charley Judge's existence in that other time?]

"Nineteen fifty-four to 1987. A.D."

[Ah. Well, from that time, 1987, you came directly to now—to early summer of this year. You had no lifetime in between; you have no other identity today. You were being no one here until your recent remarkable arrival.]

"You mean I ceased to exist? That for three million years I wasn't alive?"

[Not at all. There was no hiatus in your existence. You . . . took a shortcut: you came here directly from 1987. Consider yourself privileged.]

She looked to Uno, then back to me. [Now if you two will excuse us, the guardian and I must begin creation of the time probe.]

TWENTY-FOUR

My job became strictly defense planning; Uno did what ordinary time machine legwork there was. The time probe worked exactly as Diana intended, so Erolanna made others, and Uno brought the emeriti and trainees to Amodh Veri to stay. I didn't see why she didn't just have them come over without a "conductor," so to speak. There was, after all, an agreement of intention at the other end. But she said she'd tried it and it hadn't worked that way with them.

The newcomers began working with the probes, learning to use them. No one said much about what they were doing, but one of the results surprised me. I'd figured it would be heavy work—that they'd all be looking grim or something. But most of the time they looked bright and happy, and increasingly strong and confident. They did tell me it could get fairly bad sometimes while they were actually probing, but unless they screwed up, they felt good when they finished the trip.

Meanwhile Amodh Veri was a lot livelier than it had been. To the small, efficient, but unobtrusive household staff, there had been added six bright, increasingly energetic women. The oldest, Megeth, was way past a hundred, looked maybe sixty-five or seventy, and acted forty—a wise, bright-eyed forty. And audible! These telepaths loved to talk out loud.

As they worked with the probes, Erolanna, too, became more lively and outgoing, and Uno changed along with them. Yet any of them, Erolanna especially, could adjust easily to my moods when they felt it appropriate, apparently to make me comfortable. Sometimes they'd be talking about something and shut up when I came in. But they were so friendly and easy to be around that it didn't bother me.

Diana told me that when she had time, she'd develop a modified procedure so that non-telepaths could use a probe. Then she'd start me out on it, a scheduled amount of time each day.

Meanwhile, I decided that the easiest way to handle the invasion fleet was to burn it to the waterline, a practice already old when Caesar ruled Rome. So I took a gold candlestick back to 1981, sold it, and bought two five-gallon cans of gasoline and four cases of quart bottles. Then I sat in the garden and made a supply of Molotov cocktails.

I decided that while I was at it, I might as well be dramatic as well as destructive: I waited until night had fallen on the City of (now) Gilgaz Gorthog. I had forty-eight bottles of gasoline fitted with wicks. Forty-eight target ships, properly chosen and ignited, should result in destruction of most of the fleet.

It started out great. I dropped the first, and in seconds the whole midships deck was aflame. Then I hit a second, a third. . . . About the time I bombed the fourteenth, it began to rain. Rain in early July on the Mediterranean coast! I couldn't believe it! It poured! And didn't stop till the fires were out.

Well, fine, I thought. Just wait till you're at sea. The first several ships hit were more or less substantially damaged. If they'd been loaded with men and horses, and underway, it would have been chaos.

If Gorthog had any sense at all, I thought, he'd seriously consider cancelling the whole project now.

I decided to help him decide. I'd drop another now, and maybe another in an hour, and another maybe a half-hour after that. Let him know what he was up against. When the fleet sailed, we'd never let him sleep: It was just a matter of a large enough supply of gasoline and bottles.

So I picked a target and dropped another. Nothing! I couldn't have missed, I thought; maybe he'd put a shield over the harbor. Erolanna put the viewpoint close to the deck for me, and there was the broken bottle. I could even see the gas on the deckboards.

The wick must have gone out, I told myself. I'd try again. The result was the same. It was the same a third time. I wondered what would happen if I fire-bombed the city—if it would work. As soon as I had the idea, I felt Erolanna's thought: [No, Charley Judge, we will not burn the city.]

I didn't argue. I could handle it without that.

My new approach would be military. The time machine would come in only in the preparations. The ingredients would be surprise and relatively advanced weapons from the past. And redundancy: I'd have backup systems.

But there was this small nagging fear that anything I tried, Shu-Gwelth would foil.

I'd want weapons that didn't require technical servicing, technical maintenance, or technical training. I considered stealing machine guns, but decided artillery would be as deadly and have a bigger psychological impact on Gorthog's troops. Something of maybe Civil War vintage, easy to use at close range.

Preferably from a time/place where some cannon disappearing wouldn't cause a big upset or influence the result of some historical battle or war. Or get me shot in the process.

I had an area of the palace grounds paved—thick concrete on a bed of gravel—and Erolanna laid out a big time diagram on it with a rhombus large enough to receive almost anything I might want to bring across.

With the new diagram, my subsequent trips to see Thelmar were quick pre-dawn time trips on horseback, setting down a short distance outside Gel-Hoveth. I wondered what Farmond would think of traveling that way, but he had such faith in the guardian and me that he didn't hesitate. And it made a change in him—upgraded his self-image substantially.

Gorthog's fleet was growing faster than we'd expected, and it seemed almost certain they'd set out by late summer. And while it would be a long trip against the prevailing westerly winds, Erolanna didn't think it would take especially long. Shu-Gwelth, she said, would see that the invasion fleet enjoyed favorable winds and mild weather.

There was a time when I wouldn't have taken her seriously. Like I said, I used to devour books and magazines late into the night. Not only *Black Belt*, but *Scientific American*. Not just *Conan the Barbarian*, but *Climates of the Earth*. In *Galaxy Science Fiction*, my favorite reading in a lot of issues had been Jerry Pournelle's science articles. So I had at least a general idea about a lot of things, including planetary circulation, different kinds of weather fronts, marine and rain-shadow effects, Coriolis force—things like that.

But I'd also seen a lot of genuine magic lately. And the sudden unseasonable rainstorm that had put out my fires and dampened my confidence was not, I was sure, a natural meteorological event.

Whatever. I was operating on limited time.

I've always enjoyed good recall of details, including historical details, and I thought I knew a place where I could get the artillery I wanted, along with powder and shot. Erolanna was time probing most of the morning, and one of the few absolutes around Amodh Veri was that you never interrupt a probe session, so I caught her at lunch.

I explained what I was looking for. "After we eat," I said, "I'd like you to get September 28, 1708 A.D. for me on the viewing sphere. At Lesnaya, Russia. Would you do that?"

"Of course, Charley Judge," she said, so when we were done eating, we went to her study together. And what I saw in the sphere, in living color, was more powerful than anything I'd ever seen in the movies—Dr. Zhivago or anything. A Swedish supply column of maybe ten or twelve thousand men, none of them actors, none of them extras, with hundreds of supply wagons and field artillery pieces, were gathered in a rough oval, in a mostly open area. Centered on a tiny Russian village, they were surrounded by pine forest, meadows, and a Russian army.

We watched for several minutes. I was supposed to be sizing up the layout, but I couldn't help getting caught up in the drama and watching the fighting. It was fascinating; one of the crucial battles in the development of the world as I'd known it. The Russian forces, wearing red of all things, occupied positions mostly in the timber, pouring

artillery fire into the Swedish positions from behind hastily felled trees. A large force of Swedes,
wearing yellow and blue, were attacking out of
one side of their defensive perimeter into heavy
Russian musket fire.

Erolanna adjusted the view continually accord-
ing to my interest and attention, which she followed telepathically, so we focused and moved in
on the Swedish attack. As I watched, a section of
the Russian line was collapsing, lead elements of
the Swedish force overrunning it with fixed bayo-
nets, but in the teeth of a determined counterattack
by Russian reserves.

There were a whole lot of bodies strewn around
already. And back there somewhere was Peter the
Great, the brilliant, thoroughly unconventional emperor who was making Russia into a world power.
I'd love to get a look at him, I thought.

"Have you seen what you need to see?" Erolanna
asked. That was a nudge, I realized. She knew I
was rubbernecking.

"Sorry," I said. "Move higher; let me see the
Swedish positions again. . . . Okay, closer." Within
the Swedish perimeter I could see a number of
small, tarpaulin-covered wagons—carts, actually—
loaded with cannon balls, drawn together in a few
locations. Others of similar size were loaded with
grapeshot. The powder wagons were much larger.

"Take me ahead to nightfall." And in the sphere
it was suddenly night. Just as the military histo-
ries had described, snow was falling thickly. I could
hear scattered shooting, but this was no battle
now; it had been called on account of weather.

We had to take a viewpoint inside the Swedish
lines, right down among the men, to see much in
the thickness of large wet flakes. Three or four
inches already covered the ground and wagons. In

the darkness men were furiously digging pits, standing to their ankles in clay and water; that was where Lewenhaupt planned to bury his artillery and cannon balls. Whips smacked the rumps of horses straining to reposition heavy wagons in the sticky, snow-covered Russian mud. In one direction fire already glowed through the descending whiteness. Soldiers strode or scurried, looking grim or anxious or furtive. Officers shouted orders. At two points we saw men rummaging in what seemed to be officers' baggage wagons, handing down basket-wrapped bottles of liquor; the famed Swedish discipline was slipping.

All in all, it was a scene of semi-orderly confusion, made to order for me. Usual actions and responsibilities had been dropped; all attention and effort were concentrated on the emergency. The Swedes were preparing to fight their way out, traveling light, but first they would destroy or bury everything they could not take with them.

If some cannon disappeared, who would notice? Their crews were digging pits. Visibility was minimal. And no one was looking around; their attention was locked on whatever they were doing.

"Okay," I said, "I've seen enough."

I needed a Swedish uniform, so we went back to the no man's land across which we'd seen the Swedes attack. In the middle of it was an island of young pines, their trunks splintered and ragged from musket balls and grapeshot; the ground was strewn with Swedish dead. I selected a time when the storm had begun and the fighting had ceased. The open field was white, but under the dense canopy of treetops, little snow had yet penetrated. In the Russian lines along the main body of forest, the woodswise peasant soldiers, taciturn in the premature snowstorm, were rigging shelters. Between them and the outlying grove hung a curtain of concealing white.

We returned the view to the grove and its still largely snow-free corpses and she put me down there. Under the trees was privacy and dark silence, and the presences of the dead lingering near their bodies. I was looking for head wounds, although a bullet-holed shirt and jacket would be acceptable if there wasn't too much blood. The bodies were mostly smaller than mine—men averaged shorter in that time—but I soon found one who looked tall enough. A big-shouldered peasant, he'd long since ceased to be a player, had become a pawn. Now he was a dead pawn, the top of his blond head gone. Murmuring apology, I stripped him, put someone else's hat on my head, and Erolanna snatched me back. I wasn't feeling the greatest, but it was all right.

And even the boots fitted decently.

My skin wasn't the ideal color, but in the night-bound nightmare confusion of desperate men where I would operate, I hoped to go unchallenged if not totally unnoticed. And among those dozen thousand Swedes would surely be at least two or three or half a dozen blacks, perhaps off some foreign ships, who'd ended up in the army of Charles XII, the warrior king of Sweden.

Being there in the Swedish position was a lot different than seeing it in the sphere. Besides noise and confusion, there was a tangible *feeling*, a mixture of purpose and determination and fear that existed as itself, apart from its reflection in the faces and movements of men.

A dozen feet away a number of field pieces waited for a hole being dug. I walked in among them and

lay an arm on the brass barrel of one. Erolanna
snatched me back, and there I stood outside the
palace with the snow-coated cannon beside me.
Kilted guardsmen stood bug-eyed and slack-jawed.

"Take it away!" I ordered. As soon as they had
pushed it from the rhombus, I nodded to Erolanna
and she sent me back. After three guns, I tried a
tall-wheeled cart of cannon balls and had to wait
while the guardsmen hitched a team of horses to it
to clear the rhombus. When I got back with another cannon, Ranzil had tried a ball down a muzzle to be sure they were the right size.

Before I was done, I'd spent a long and exhausting
Ixmatl morning in four or five minutes of Russian
night. Twenty-five field pieces stood on the palace
grounds, plus two carts of cannon balls, two of
grapeshot, and two powder wagons.

But before I went to clean up, I had Erolanna
skip ahead; I wanted to see the action to its finish.
The snowfall had thinned considerably. Thousands
of Swedes were moving down the road against
little resistance, the infantry riding on wagon horses.
Abandoned wagons and empty gun carriages burned
tall in the night.

The faces we looked into were mostly pretty
alert now. The adrenalin was acting, and there
was hope, even confidence, now that they were
relieved of the burden of mud-bound wagons. But
burned and buried behind them was the hope of
the main army. And I knew what they did not—
that many would be killed or captured the next
day, that most of the rest would lose their lives or
their freedom at Poltava the next summer, and in
between, many would lose fingers and toes to the
worst European winter in then-living memory.

It really *had* been a lousy game on Weirro/Earth/

Ixmatl—a game rigged to lose. And we'd been losing it for one hundred and fifty thousand generations.

Thelmar sent men to be trained on the guns. I gave them quite a lot of target practice—enough that, before we were done, I went back again to that snowy Russian night and got several more carts of balls and shot as well as six more powder wagons.

Meanwhile, Gorthog's fleet had sailed—three hundred and sixty ships with approximately fifteen thousand soldiers, averaging about forty per ship. If that doesn't sound like a lot per ship, keep in mind that these were little wooden tubs, and that the whole army was cavalry; there were about forty horses on each one, too. And feed, and bedding, and weapons.

One bad storm could be a disaster for them, but it didn't look like that was going to happen. Because it seemed that Gorthog really did control the wind. Even Erolanna couldn't believe the speed his fleet was making; the three thousand-plus miles were shrinking fast.

And by comparison, my twenty-five cannon and Thelmar's twenty-one hundred soldiers looked more and more paltry.

I'd renamed my new horse "Arrow;" I was sensitive lately about wind. We were out alone, Arrow and I, and I was thinking about additional possibilities. It was a lovely day, and I was getting some loafing done along with the thinking. The sun was shining; there was a slight breeze; the field clover was in bloom, and a stringer of woods lay glossy green in a draw to my left.

Maybe, maybe, I thought, a couple of cases of

M-16's, a couple of ammo, and two or three of grenades could be arranged. Earlier, after some mulling, I'd decided to bring a light anti-personnel tank through; it would have fitted in the rhombus, and I knew how to operate it. But it wouldn't come over. I tried, and it insisted on staying in 1987. I had a sneaking suspicion that subconsciously I had an unwillingness to do it. So maybe, if push came to shove, I'd try it again and it would work.

Or maybe Diana and company, probing around in the agreement area, would come up with something that would simply result in the invasion being abandoned. But my job was doing, not wishing.

I thought about rock bombs. It was one thing for Shu-Gwelth to cause my wicks to go out, but it would be something else to stop fifty-pound blocks of stone, released above his anti-magic shield. They'd make quite a hole in those little wooden ships.

I didn't know how high the shield extended; it might take respectable aiming to hit them. But it seemed feasible, and with a fleet that large, almost surely many of the ships would be outside the shield. First I'd have to find quarries with the right sized rocks; I wasn't willing to rob a graveyard. Or maybe I could use engine blocks from an automobile plant. We could set them on slings in the garden, and then . . .

Wild whinnying a ways off caught my attention. A horse, a quarter mile ahead, was charging up the slope near the head of the draw. Arrow was immediately nervous, snorting, trying to turn back; he really wanted to get away from there. I reined him in while keeping my eyes on the distant horse, which was kicking wildly now with his hind hooves.

Then it went down, with the damndest bleating I ever imagined from a horse. My hair stood on end. I grabbed hobbles and picket pin from a saddlebag, got down and hobbled and picketed Arrow. The hide on his rump and shoulders was twitching. Then I trotted toward the strange horse on foot.

But I didn't go all the way. At a couple of hundred feet I could see what had happened; a swirl of bees were flying around the animal, whose prone body had all but stopped jerking. They sent a couple of scouts my way, pretty antagonistic, so I stopped and played it cool, and they buzzed off.

Down the slope, where I'd first noticed the horse, was a large patch thick with clover. The horse had gone there to feed, and so had the bees, who probably had a hive in a hollow tree in the woods just below. In thick clover like that, there had probably been hundreds of bees working the blossoms. The horse had offended one of them, gotten stung, probably crow-hopped around and made some more mad at him and gotten stung several more times.

Then he had panicked—that's when I'd noticed him—they'd smelled the panic, and every other bee in the clover patch had gone for him. And they'd killed him.

I remembered a friend in high school who'd had her horse killed by bees. She damn near died in the hospital herself. All that saved her was that the panicked horse had unloaded her and the medics had treated her with anti-venom in time. She'd been riding through an orchard in bloom and there'd been a hive not far away.

I was very thoughtful, riding back to Amodh Veri.

TWENTY-FIVE

The sky was a great blue bowl inverted over a darker blue sea. Two miles ahead and closing was the vast fleet of Gilgaz Gorthog. Our own little flotilla was beating southward against the wind; closure was mainly from the invading fleet riding down the wind toward us.

The weather was beautiful. It felt as if there should be excursion boats on the sidelines—women wearing long gowns and carrying parasols, and gentlemen with bowler hats, all waiting to enjoy the spectacle.

It did look to be a spectacle pending, not a contest, with an open line of twenty-four small ships arrayed against a mass of three-hundred-sixty, or fifteen to one. But each of ours had a stinger in its tail, a cannon swivel-mounted on a stern platform. When we were near enough, we'd put about and run ahead of them, letting them look down our muzzles. Our gunners were competent, our captains and crews well drilled in their maneuvers.

I'd had two main concerns. If Gorthog knew we planned to come out and do battle, he might have hit our flotilla with a savage squall. Apparently, he hadn't known, or maybe he considered us too feeble to trouble with. Now we were so close that a storm which hit us would hit them too. I hoped.

My other concern had been sea monsters, like the one in Urigwerm's pool, but none had shown. I wasn't that surprised. I'd run into an interesting item of lore from, of all people, Thelmar. It had been said of Urigwerm that "he could command water, wind, and fire." There'd been nothing there about commanding life. What I'd seen in Urigwerm's pool was probably an infertile freak, perhaps the product of some sorcerous messing around with octopus embryos, a solitary phenomenon displayed to visitors for psychological effects. At any rate, each of our ships had half a dozen men with heavy broadswords razor sharp, whose primary function was to chop off encroaching tentacles.

I wasn't actually part of flotilla command; I'd just dropped in on the flagship. Commodore Jarok and his crew were familiar with my appearances and disappearances. And despite the size of the enemy fleet, I found the men not only confident but eager.

"There's a many of 'em," Jarok commented drily, watching the oncoming armada. His eyes were narrow chinks in a leathery face, long years adapted to wind and the glare of sun on sea. "I'm glad they're not spread out wide; I'd not want 'em to flank us."

"Just don't try to get too close," I said. "We don't want them closer than half a cable after you've turned."

"Aye. Though I'm not expecting 'em to try running us down. Not after we start shooting. They'll be dropping sail in hopes we'll leave 'em behind."

Could very well be, I thought, unless Gorthog came up with something unforeseen. From past performance, he was not a versatile sorcerer. He had his shield against magic, could control water, wind, and fire in his immediate locale, and he was a telepath. But he seemed to rely mainly on conventional physical actions and his ability to influence the decisions of others.

If he had any further magical tricks up his sleeve, I'd no doubt know about them soon.

The enemy was drawing rapidly nearer. They must be wondering now, perhaps even feeling a little uncomfortable about why we kept coming. I'd have liked to stay, but I had other things to do.

Jarok made it easy for me. "Shouldn't you be getting back to the farm?" he asked. I nodded, signalled Erolanna, and she snatched me to the big outdoor diagram—the one we were using for defense. Nearby stood row upon row of beehives, each enclosed in a small tent of muslin netting and resting on a wooden pallet with handles for carrying.

I ignored them now and went to the stand on which the viewing sphere rested. Erolanna was watching it.

"Morale is good down there," I commented. "They're going to cause quite an effect."

She nodded, eyes intent on the sphere. The little line of gunships were hardly a mile from the enemy. I didn't know whether the crews were getting nervous, but I was. The distance shrank to one thousand yards, eight-hundred, six-hundred. Finally at maybe four-hundred yards they started to come about; my stomach was a knot. By the time they had their sterns to the invaders, no more than one hundred and fifty yards separated them from the leading enemy ships. They'd carried out their evolution surprisingly well, considering that only five were actually Thelmar's "navy"—actually more of a coast guard. The others were merchant ships, drafted with their crews.

The distance closed to less than a hundred yards before they picked up full downwind speed, and it was then old Jarok fired his gun. It was a great opening shot—the charge of grape swept the deck of a pursuer; many of the men topside went down, and she began to swerve with no one at the tiller.

The sound of the shot triggered a ragged volley from the others, and almost at once, several stricken ships began to come about with their helmsmen dead or down. Three or four others were losing headway, falling back; their sails had swung loose as if rigging had been severed and their booms freed.

The others came on, though—I doubt if any of them really understood what was happening—and our gunners recharged their pieces. The flagship fired again, and a continual series of cannon shots could be heard up and down the line. In a minute or two, a number of pursuers began to come about, some to avoid collisions with others out of control, some simply in confusion.

Jarok switched to ball then, and shortly, others followed suit. As the distance widened between fleets, Jarok, too, came about, the others following irregularly. Several of the enemy seemed to be taking water. Several had collided. More were dropping sail to fall back. A few had come completely about-ship and were trying to tack southward through the oncoming fleet. Confusion was a chain reaction.

The action continued for more than an hour; then Jarok disengaged and sailed his flotilla north-ward unpursued, its supply of balls and shot depleted. Some twenty enemy ships were awash or settling in the water. Twice that number were drifting, rigging dangling or masts down. Many had been holed above waterline, and their casualties were surely numerous.

I turned to Ranzil and nodded toward the hives. "Okay," I said, "let's do it."

Two nervous-looking guardsmen picked up the end hive in the nearest row and carried it carefully to the rhombus. The occupants droned ominously inside their delicate tent. I put my attention on one of the uncrippled enemy ships and Erolanna put the viewpoint about ten feet above the companionway opening amidships.

"Now," I told her, and the hive in the rhombus disappeared, to fall through the opening into the ship's hold.

"Bullseye!" I shouted, and all hell broke loose below deck. The ruptured hive had loosed not two-hundred or five-hundred, but thousands of infuriated bees. We could hear the screaming of horses and men. Soldiers erupted onto the deck, arms swinging frenziedly, coated with bees and pursued by a cloud of others. Those on deck were also quickly found and attacked; most managed to leap overboard. I doubt if any who'd been below deck survived; most never made it out of the hold. Many who jumped quickly drowned. Even those who could swim were sporadically attacked.

I flapped an arm at Erolanna, and white-faced, she withdrew the viewpoint. I was shaking! It had not occurred to me that it would be so terrible to see. After that we'd drop a hive and jerk back the viewpoint at once.

Over the next several hours we dropped a hundred and thirteen hives, then stopped. We had only a few left; I was holding them in reserve in a clover field a mile away, their occupants free and contentedly making honey. We'd bring them in the next night.

Actually, I'd stolen well over three hundred hives of bees. Farmond and I spent a number of nights stealing commercial hives from the twentieth century. We wore stolen protective clothing and worked in the cool, dark, predawn hours when the bees were quiescent. We'd put a hive on a stolen pallet inside a crude frame of stolen lumber and nails, cover it with a tent of stolen netting using a stolen spring-driven stapler, and bring it through.

Sound simple? But there were also the hours spent, lots of them, finding farms with the hives isolated enough, and in different regions and times, to avoid alarming the beekeepers and risking armed guards being set. And there was the job of stealing the pallets and the linoleum we used to make the pallets bee-proof. And stealing the lumber and nails for the frames, and even getting enough claw hammers. I'd worried about getting them built right by a peasant crew, but Bressir bossed the job, with Ranzil's backing, and it got done.

I'm not sure what went wrong; I'm not up on bee pathology. Maybe we confined the bees too long, or maybe the netting reduced the circulation in the tents too much in the hot, humid weather we were having just then. But most of the hives were wiped out by some disease. We'd kept bringing more until the last night, to make up as many of the losses as possible. And instead of having enough for most of the ships, we had about a third enough.

I couldn't help but think I should have gone with the stone bomb idea then. I even told Diana and Erolanna that I wanted to drop back three weeks in the time machine and warn myself; I'd keep preparing over and over again until I got it right. But neither of them would go for it. Erolanna said it could introduce unpredictable bad effects into present time.

I'd have argued with her; what bad effects could be worse than facing an overwhelming force with seriously inadequate resources? But she had Diana's agreement, so I'd backed off.

I'd been grim and tired when I'd finally quit for a few hours of sleep before the battle.

Gorthog's flagship had survived; he was traveling beneath his anti-magic shield. It didn't have the extent of the umbrella that had protected Urigwerm's castle, fortunately. Maybe it was the same sort of problem some earlier guardians had had in operating on the move. But the shield was there. When I'd tried to bee-bomb his flagship, the hive fell into the water about two hundred yards away.

For some time the fleet lay in widely scattered disarray, some ships circling, others floating with sails furled. A handful had fled south. About a third drifted derelict, coffins for horses and men. I was hoping to see the flagship turn and head for home then, and after about an hour they began to regroup at a distance from the derelicts.

But when they took a heading again, it was northward. The invasion was still on, with about two hundred ships and seven or eight thousand cavalry. Morale must have been out the bottom— surely fear would be the prevalent emotion on board—but we were still in serious trouble. Once they recovered a bit, they'd start thinking about revenge. And those were soldiers who'd conquered most of the Middle East.

That evening the fleet passed the mouth of Bregh-Sreumedh without entering, which confirmed that the invaders were going to land at Blue River and strike Amodh Veri first. Thelmar ordered fifteen hundred ready cavalry on a forced march through the night on the road to Blue River.

With that news, I crashed for a good long night's sleep, so tired I didn't even dream of bees.

TWENTY-SIX

I spent all the next day getting ready for the day after that. Jarok helped by harassing and slowing the fleet with what powder and ball he had left, holding only a little back for emergency.

I made a hurried pickup with the time machine— as hurried as the job allowed—going back to Tunis in 1945, where I scouted out contacts and picked up 300 pounds of TNT, a box of percussion caps, and 400 yards of primacord. And I *bought* the damned stuff! On the black market. Got them to throw in a .303 Enfield rifle and a bando- lier of cartridges, too. The Arabs had stolen the stuff from the British Eighth Army.

At first I thought they were trying to cheat me, because the primacord was the wrong color. But they demonstrated a few feet of it, and it was the real stuff—fuse that burns so fast it amounts to a slow explosion. Apparently, the British color-coded theirs differently than we did in the States.

I told them to stack it all on a rug and I'd be back with the gold in a few minutes. I figured they'd follow me, so I ducked into an alley and signaled Erolanna. It must have puzzled hell out of them to find me disappeared.

They were also puzzled at the strange coinage I brought back with me. While they were cutting and examining a couple of pieces for fraud, I went over to the stack of ordnance, knelt on the rug beside it, and disappeared with it right in front of them.

I could have taken it without paying, of course, but I was sick and tired of ripping people off.

Late that night, Ingoth Klar arrived with his army. He'd driven them hard all the way, with only two short sleeping breaks, but if they were less than fresh, they were still functional. I made them ride another hour so they'd be where they were needed, with two of Erolanna's guardsmen along to stand watch for them when they got there. I didn't trust Klar's men to stay awake on watch.

Me—I didn't think I was sleepy anymore; too wound up. But Diana wasn't there—we'd evacuated her with some of the others—so I couldn't bend her ear. So I went back to bed anyway and was asleep before I finished lying down.

The first of Gorthog's ships entered the harbor a little before sunup. They'd put a force of about two hundred men ashore on the south headland, and these entered the town cautiously, where they encountered detachments of Klar's army. Klar's troops let them take the waterfront area, as wanted, but restricted them to it. When invader horsemen had control of the streets near the wharf, they signaled the fleet by setting fire to a building, and fifteen of their larger ships moved in to dock.

By the time the fifteenth had tied up, troops from the first several had moved out to reinforce their defensive perimeter, and others were forming up into units on the waterfront road. The first ship was preparing to cast off. That's when I dropped in with a lighted fusee in my hand and lit the primacord. The charges I'd set all along the wharf, just above waterline, went off like a string of giant ladyfingers; I heard the first few before Erolanna pulled me back, and the whole series at Amodh Veri via the sphere, offset in time a second or so.

Disaster City! Do you have any idea what 300 pounds of TNT can do? Or what it sounds like? Even in thirty separate charges? It would be bad enough if you were prepared and experienced. But for those people . . . Not many who were still on board lived to get off, and the ships began to sink at once. The troops forming up on the road were protected from the blasts by the wharf, which was only the shore built up and reinforced by timbers. But still they were so deafened and stunned that they didn't notice or didn't react to the rumble of Klar's cavalry. A lot of their horses had gone down from the enormous roar. Even the defensive perimeter was confused and distracted, and quickly overrun; it was more of a massacre than a fight. Those who escaped the sword by jumping into the bay were used for target practice, unless they drowned first. The casualties must have been somewhere around a thousand.

And the wharf was blocked to further landings by a line of ships sitting on the bottom in water up to their bulwarks.

It took only a few minutes to see what they'd do next. After some signaling from the flagship, the ships that had been waiting their turns at the wharf raised anchor. But not to leave. They crossed the narrow bay, re-anchored near the far shore, and their troops began to disembark. The hard way, by riding their blindfolded horses through the gangways, plunging into the water. As most of the ships had only about five or six feet of freeboard amidships, not too many men drowned. Units quickly began to form up on the marshy shore.

I looked at Erolanna and she at me. I wasn't eager, but it was time for the next act. Besides a breastplate, I wore a steel cap, with the nasal removed for optimum visibility. But my real protection was my skill and Erolanna's quickness.

I stepped into the rhombus and came out swinging, into the rear of a group of invaders. It took them about eight or ten bloody seconds before they began to get it together, and at that moment a watchful guardian angel snatched me back. I was spattered with crimson from helmet to boots, fortunately all of it other people's.

"Out there," attention was in the direction of the noisy fight I'd just left, so we put me down on the other side of the group, and again I laid into them from behind. This time I got in only about five or six seconds work before she pulled me.

A straightforward fight they were willing to have, but my will-o'-the-wisp act left them bug-eyed and looking nervously around. Life and death these last few days seemed a function of sorcery and utterly out of their control. But then an officer had them mount and wait in the saddle, and they felt a little better.

Moments later they began to move out, riding along the bay toward the river. Presumably, they'd ride upstream far enough to ford without a long swim. And I wanted to do as much damage as possible while they were still on that side. Without using the few beehives I had held in reserve.

I turned to the waiting guardsmen. "Let's have it," I said, and they pushed the field gun to the rhombus, the one cannon I'd withheld from the flotilla. It was already charged with grapeshot, and fitted with a homemade iron shield so I'd have some protection while aiming.

The ground where I'd appear was soft, and I wouldn't be able to turn the gun, so I stood looking along the barrel, intending to come through facing the enemy. Good old intention, the number one ingredient: When I appeared, the barrel was pointed right at them, about sixty yards away. I lowered it a little and fired. She roared and jumped, and Erolanna pulled me back. While guardsmen reloaded, I examined the result through the sphere. About a dozen horses were down and a couple of others riderless. But the biggest effect was the confusion: Forward motion had been converted to milling around. It was about a minute before their officers got them shouted and cursed eastward again.

The next time I wasn't quite as lucky. I had to adjust the elevation more, which took a few seconds. I heard an arrow strike the shield, and one came through the barrel slot, narrowly missing me as I reached to fire. Again she boomed and bucked, and back at Amodh Veri I listened with Erolanna to the reverberations.

The third time, several of the enemy charged when I appeared. I didn't wait to adjust elevation—just touched her off and left. Three of the four that charged me were in the line of fire and got blown away; the fourth bailed out of the saddle. But this time there was no milling around in the ranks; after a momentary pause, they kept going.

We checked the landing beach again. Men continued to come ashore, and would for a while. The new arrivals weren't alerted to me yet, so I decided to pay them a visit. I didn't realize they'd rowed Gilgaz Gorthog ashore. His shield was functioning; when Erolanna went to set me down again, I got dumped in a reed-grown slough maybe two hundred yards away. Fortunately, the enemy didn't notice; it would have made me look ridiculous, and image was important to our strategy.

Before long, and with a few dozen more casualties from yours truly, their lead elements were upstream far enough to ford it. Ingoth Klar's cavalry demonstrated on the far shore, discouraging a crossing until enough invaders had gathered to do it successfully against resistance. Meanwhile, I used some longer range gunnery from outside Gorthog's shield. But the range was long for grape, and solid balls aren't that effective on personnel.

When they were ready, they crossed, under heavy archery from Klar's men, taking heavy losses. But they never faltered. There was brief fighting on the south bank; then Klar's trumpeter blew, and his men rode off under cover of mounted bowmen.

And the enemy was on our side of the river now, in numbers that would soon be overwhelming. We'd counted our last big coup at the wharf; we'd shot our wad. Despair swelled in my gut. I realized that, since then, all my bopping in and out had amounted to trivial sniping: I'd been wasting precious time. And I couldn't see what to do next.

So I ordered bread and cheese and buttermilk, and ate lunch in the garden, alone. After that I returned to watch with Erolanna at the sphere.

I had this urge to snap and swear at the people around me. But the fact was, and I knew it, they'd done everything I'd asked them to, and it was actually remarkable how little had been screwed up. The biggest screwup had been losing so many beehives. And that had been my fault, however it happened. If only I had three more days! *If only, if only.* The two most useless words in the world.

Next to *it's all your fault.* But if only I had another hundred hives. Or been able to bring the tank through. Why hadn't I? Why hadn't it worked?

I was tired, my head ached, and I wanted to go crawl in a hole and pull the dirt in after me.

We'd done incredibly well, but fallen far short. There were probably no more than six thousand invaders left, out of an initial fifteen thousand, but six thousand were enough. Not for Europe, but for Gel-Leneth. And my job had been to keep Amodh Veri secure, not to fail nobly or magnificently.

That still was my job, and I had maybe an hour and a half left to accomplish it.

Amodh Veri was largely empty now. Diana, Uno, the two "younger" emeriti, and the trainees had been transported to the mountains with most of the household staff and guardsmen. Old Megeth had stayed, prepared to transport Erolanna and the rod of knowledge at the last minute if necessary, to keep them out of Gorthog's hands.

That would set the time probe project back seriously and leave us without a time diagram for dealing with defense and procurement problems. Which was intolerable. And it would leave Shu-Gwelth and his army with a major victory.

Meanwhile, I didn't have those hundred hives, but I had six, vigorous and hostile. I could hear them.

The whole army was across now, and I watched Gorthog split it into two forces. About four thousand started downstream, I assumed to besiege Cratlik's castle. Maybe he thought the guardian might have taken refuge there; otherwise, it made no sense. The other two thousand or so started up out of the valley toward Amodh Veri.

Gorthog himself was with the smaller force, riding near the lead elements but far enough back to

be protected from possible cannon attack by a
mass of mounted soldiers. Erolanna put the viewpoint about twenty feet above his head and we
dropped a cannonball. Not so much to see if we
could kill him with it as to test the shield. I have
no idea where the ball landed, but obviously the
shield was functioning.

We tried it again from fifty feet; same result.
Somewhere overhead the shield must end, I was
sure of that, and a hive dropped from above it
would penetrate, because it would be under the
force of gravity, not magic. Back at the Inner Sea,
I'd penetrated Shu-Gwelth's shield with a rowboat
as if it hadn't been there. But a hive dropped from
above fifty feet—two hundred feet or whatever—
would smash down so hard that the bees would
almost surely be killed. In which case it would
only do the job if it actually hit Gorthog directly.

"Farmond!" I snapped, "go get—go get the curtains from the French doors in the guardian's room.
Run!"

I turned to Ranzil. "Where is some strong cord
around here that isn't thick and rope-like?"

He thought for an interminable few seconds.
"Now!" I said sharply.

"Uh, yes! Old Gwindor, the stable master, used
to fish with set lines in the river." He began to be
excited. "He used a long stout linen cord, with
short lines attached!"

"Where?" I demanded. "Where is it?"

"I saw it just the other day, on a spool in—"

"Get it," I said, "as fast as you can!" He turned
and ran from the room.

I needed to know how high the shield extended;
I had neither time nor material for mistakes. I
wanted to make the drop from as low as possible
so there wouldn't be time for Gorthog to gallop

out of the danger zone if he spotted the parachute coming down. At the same time I didn't want to test any further with cannonballs. Drop a cannonball from above the shield and they'd be looking at the sky from then on.

So I had myself transported into the back room of a pet shop I knew in Fayetteville, North Carolina, near Bragg, went in front and picked up a cage with two canaries, then into the back room again and home. A dead bird falling out of the sky would not hold much attention. Two hundred and fifty feet proved high enough, which was a lot better than I'd been afraid it might be.

The invader force was only a mile and a half from Amodh Veri by the time I was ready. I held one crude parachute up over the hive with a guardsman's pike, with Farmond and Ranzil holding the other two from just outside the rhombus, using brooms. I wanted to be damned sure they all opened in the short distance they'd have. Erolanna was the bombardier again.

It disappeared. Quickly I stepped beside her, the few others crowding around the sphere in a small ring. The hive was so beautiful, swinging slightly beneath its chutes as it descended. I counted the seconds to myself—"*four* thousand, *five* thousand, *six* . . . I don't believe anyone near the emperor even noticed it until I'd gotten to ten thousand, when it was only maybe fifty feet above the ground.

It was Gorthog himself who looked up. I could see his startled expression, but he didn't try to spur his horse away. Maybe he didn't realize what it was. It hit and broke apart about twelve feet in front of him.

I gave us about six seconds to cheer, then snapped orders. I knew the troops would scatter, and I needed to be sure that none of them came galloping on to Amodh Veri. We had the cannon ready, rolled it onto the rhombus, put some clusters of grape beside it, some powder, wadding, and the ramrod. Then Farmond and I added ourselves to the cargo and Erolanna set us down between Amodh Veri and a loose aggregation of soldiers galloping toward it. I fired once, and that was all it took. They weren't jammed up, so only two of the leaders went down, but they knew the cannon by now, and the others swerved and rode off more or less at right angles. We reloaded and fired twice more, hurriedly, and others coming farther back also turned away. Then Erolanna picked us up.

The sphere showed maybe forty dead horses in the drop zone, but many more had surely been stung and bolted, maybe to die farther off. There were somewhat more human bodies than horse bodies, as if they'd been thrown by their panicked horses. The bulk of the regiment, having been behind the emperor, had stampeded back down the road. Now many of them had stopped, uncertain what to do next. I helped them decide by dropping another hive just in front of them, and they fled on down the road with no further hesitation, leaving another two acres of scattered dead behind them.

But the situation wasn't handled yet. There were still some enemy horsemen vagrant in the vicinity, too dangerous to have hanging around. With the Enfield rifle I'd gotten from the Arabs—an old bolt-action weapon—I rode Arrow into the rhombus and onto the meadow about two hundred feet from two of them.

"Halloo!" I called. "Go back to your ships!"

They stopped and looked at me, and I could see one of them say something. He took his short bow from its boots and reached back over his shoulder for an arrow. I raised the rifle and fired, and he pitched from his saddle. His buddy glanced down at him, then at me, and spurred his horse northwestward toward the bay. I spent the next half hour routing stragglers, shooting eight and running off maybe twenty. When I was done, the immediate threat to Amodh Veri was over. But there was an army of four thousand only seven miles away, around Cratlik's castle. And it seemed like I'd better get them moving back to the bay, too. When you've got them on the run, keep them running.

Meanwhile, I knew I was operating on an empty tank, emotionally, but I wasn't going to let down when victory seemed within reach.

TWENTY-SEVEN

Invaders formed a ring around Cratlik's castle. A lot of the four thousand were actually in town, tearing down buildings for timbers to make siege engines. And already some of the group we'd repelled near Amodh Veri were straggling in to join them.

I really didn't want to kill anymore if I had a choice; from a purely practical point of view, there were too many to kill with the resources at hand, anyway. So I went back and picked up Gorthog's body. The bees were mostly off him by then, and I brushed off what were left with my hand. Most of them coated the wreckage of the hive in a strange, lethargic, furry mass—a lot of them dead, apparently. I didn't even see one flying.

Bees are strange and interesting creatures.

Then we dropped the corpse into the middle of the besieging army. I thought they might quit when they saw it, but they didn't. They still were that organism called an army, with its parts depending on the head. And they had a new head—one they'd long known and had confidence in—their General Terzuk. I remembered hearing him mentioned by Santho when I was in the dungeon.

They were thousands of miles from home, their ships didn't seem very safe, if Terzuk said, "Boys, we're staying and conquering this place," they stayed, and at least tried to conquer.

Next we looked for Ingoth Klar. He was with his army, cooking a meal in the woods about five miles away. Erolanna set me down beside him.

"Klar!" I said. "I didn't expect to find you here."

He scowled. "Where did you expect us?"

"I thought you'd be harassing the enemy."

"To what avail? Against such an army, we can save neither guardian nor anything else in Cratlik's district. I went further than I should have in sending eighty men to reinforce his people at the castle. And Amodh Veri is impossible to defend.

"No, we are going to Gel-Hoveth to defend the king and the city."

"Okay," I said, "I got all that. But Gorthog is dead now and we have driven the enemy away from Amodh Veri with magic. What we want now is your help in driving them out of the country all together."

He shook his head stubbornly. "There are not enough of us. We are going to Gel-Hoveth. There are more troops there, and an armed and drilled militia."

I let it go at that—wished him good luck and disappeared. Arguing would only waste time.

And told Erolanna to put me down right next to Terzuk. If I killed him, maybe then the army would pick up and leave. She was calm, her gaze as clear as it had been all day long, her old sober look outgrown since she'd been probing. I stepped into the rhombus, sword in hand, and nodded.

But she didn't send me. "You're not ready," she said. "Put your attention on what you're about to do."

The words jolted me. It would be suicidal to go into that scene down there with my head up my ass. My eyes went to the sphere again, and then to a mental holograph I created in the rhombus with me.

And abruptly I was there. With zero hesitation I struck Terzuk, my daito cutting through his thick neck like a pot roast, and at that same instant, someone hit me from behind. I turned, aware that something was terribly wrong with my left arm, and slashed one-handed, once, twice, and realized I was falling.

I woke up in a hospital bed and looked around. I was in a ward, and this was very definitely not Ixmatl. A nurse was taking someone's temperature a few beds away. On a wall was an electric clock with a red sweep hand making its routine inspection of all the minute/second marks. I realized I was wearing a body cast.

Faintly I could hear traffic.

"Nurse," I said. It didn't have much behind it.

She looked over at me and grinned. Like Erolanna's, her hair was copper red. "Our mysterious stranger!" she said, then turned back and took the thermometer from the guy's mouth. She wrote something down on a clipboard, then came over to me.

"Where am I?" I asked.

"Presbyterian Hospital."

"Presbyterian Hospital where? What city?"

Her eyebrows arched. "Toronto."

Very cautiously I asked, "What's the date?"

"May fifteenth."

That hardly helped. It was hard to ask the next question. "What—what year?"

Her face was abruptly serious. My condition, she

decided, went deeper than they'd thought. "Nine-teen eighty-seven," she said.

I wanted to cry. *Somehow,* I thought, *I've done it again. I've time-jumped on my own. And she'll never find me here. I've lost her.*

The nurse was not the hand-patting kind. She told me to open my mouth, and stuck a thermometer in it, effectively gagging me, then left. Three minutes later she was back with a doctor.

I'd been there a day and a half, he told me. They'd found me unconscious in the emergency room, crudely bandaged and seeping blood, with no record of having been registered in.

Bandaged! Someone had bandaged me! I hadn't solo-jumped there on my own from the battlefield!

He said they needed to know my name. I lied and told him I didn't remember. Then I asked what was the matter with me. A massive cut, he said, a broken shoulder blade and broken ribs. "It looked," he went on, "as if someone had hacked you with a sword or a machete. Not an everyday sort of injury."

He was watching me closely as he said it, so I looked vaguely surprised. *I know where you can find a lot of injuries like that,* I thought. *On the south bank of the Blue River.* Meanwhile, he told me that my shoulder blade was now held together with steel pins.

I had no idea what had happened, I said, and I didn't remember ever having been in Toronto until just now. "Am I going to be here quite a while?"

"Probably not. You should be able to go home in five days or a week. Assuming we can find out where home is and there's someone there to take care of you."

I didn't enlighten him. I didn't want a bed with sheets that tie down at the sides. Now and then

over the next several days I got despondent, afraid
I'd never get back to Amodh Veri. Or that I'd gone
psycho and there wasn't any Ixmatl or Erolanna,
that I'd been in some kind of martial arts brawl
and gotten dumped off here. And that all the rest
had been some strange trip from something they'd
shot me with in the hospital.

But those depressions never lasted long; I'd come
right out of it.

Another thing that bugged me off and on was,
have things gone to hell in the war, without me to
handle things? Maybe they'd dumped me for safe-
keeping, and couldn't pick me back up because
they'd fled Amodh Veri and had no time diagram
to operate with. That looked like a real possibility.

I never worried long about that either. Mostly I
caught up on my sleep, being on sedatives. The
pain was drug-dulled, the personnel mostly pretty
good, and if the hospital chow was no better than
in the States, I was still recovering nicely.

On the fourth day they took me off the sedatives,
and I started feeling brighter. I even shuffled to
the dining room to eat. The doctor had told me I
was doing exceptionally well, that tomorrow they'd
have someone from the American consulate talk to
me. They were pretty sure I was American from
the peculiar way I said certain words, like "out"
and "about." He asked me to say "aluminium,"
and when I said "You mean aluminum?", he
laughed.

That night I lay in bed, sleepless for the first
time here, trying to call Erolanna telepathically.
You know I'm here, I thought. *You must.* Someone
*bandaged me. You snatched me back, bandaged me,
and sent me here. That's the only explanation that
fits.*

No, there was another—one that I didn't like to

look at. Why was I here in Toronto? How would Erolanna know to send me somewhere where they had socialized medicine and spoke English? One answer was that she wouldn't. The most rational explanation was a martial arts brawl, followed by hallucination from the drugs they'd . . .

[Charley Judge.]

"Oh Jesus!" I said it right out loud. I hadn't realized what a relief it would be, even though it was Megeth and not Erolanna.

[Are you ready to come back?]

I grinned like a goddamn bear. [*You bet your sweet ass I'm ready,*] I thought back at her.

TWENTY-EIGHT

It was a wild and wonderful homecoming. Megeth yelled like a joyous, gray-haired banshee that I was there, and people came running and got to see a grown man cry. I mean, I was feeling great, but the tears were really flowing.

They were all there, Diana, the emeriti, everyone. Even cook came in. At first the talk was pretty chaotic, but rather quickly it sorted out to people filling me in on everything that had happened while I was gone.

They'd broken the siege without me. Erolanna had dropped a bee bomb, and some of the enemy soldiers started to sneak off down the hill to town, to hide out. That indicated something about morale, with both Gorthog and Terzuk dead. And then Farmond got this brilliant idea, and he and Ranzil put on beekeeper suits, set down in the bee area with the cannon, and began to fire charge after charge at the enemy. No one, but no one, tried to attack them there, and god knows what the enemy thought they were in their costumes. They cleared out everyone within grapeshot range. Meanwhile, Erolanna had transported Uno to talk to Thelmar, and Thelmar sat down and wrote an order to Ingoth

Klar, which Uno then delivered. Koth then grimly turned his troops around and started back toward Blue River.

After retrieving Farmond and Ranzil, she'd dropped another bee bomb where the invaders' senior surviving officers were conferring. That broke it. The soldiers began to leave en masse, heading for the bay, and none of their officers tried to stop them. In fact, when they got there, several officers took a boat, rowed awkwardly to the flagship, and apparently told them that both Gorthog and Terzuk were dead. Ships then moved close to the south shore, and soon there was a mass of men on horseback swimming out to them.

When Ingoth Klar had arrived that evening, there was no one left to fight, and many of the ships had already departed the harbor. They swept the countryside and found maybe a hundred enemy soldiers total, who'd deserted earlier and missed the departure. So again he turned his army around and headed for Gel-Hoveth.

But Farmond hadn't been satisfied; he'd been watching me operate for too long. As soon as the ships began leaving, he pointed out that they still might decide to attack Gel-Hoveth. He said that he and Ranzil should go back to the twentieth century and steal a few more hives, just in case. There were some pallets stacked up, and boards for tents, from hives that had died.

So they got them scrubbed down to avoid contamination, the way I'd had done with others we'd reused, took the last of the netting, and stole six more hives. It turned out they didn't need them; the enemy fleet never paused, but just continued for home. But it had been good thinking on Farmond's part. And the bees are happily pollinating the clover in Gel-Leneth today.

So much for worrying that they couldn't finish without me.

I watched a lot of this on the sphere the day after my return, proud as a father. But when most of it had actually been happening, I'd been lying unconscious in my room, with a fever.

When Erolanna had snatched me bleeding from the melee near Cratlik's castle, the first thing they'd tried, after getting me bandaged and the bleeding stopped, was to go back to just before the blow struck, to see if they could pull me out before I got wounded. But there wasn't more than the tiniest split second, if that, between my striking Terzuk and being hacked myself.

Then she considered sending Uno back to just before I'd gone to kill Terzuk, to warn me. But the imprint recorder indicated I was in no danger of dying, so she'd decided not to meddle with an action that promised victory. Not yet, anyway.

Then, during the enemy exodus to the bay, she took time to bring Diana and the other refugees back to Amodh Veri. The first thing Diana did was to contact me telepathically right through the unconsciousness. I replied telepathically in my "sleep," saying nothing on my own of course, but answering her questions. Out of that came the decision to transport me to Toronto.

They'd intended to keep in telepathic communication with me if they could, so I wouldn't worry, using the sphere to help make the contact. But the sedative the hospital put me on dulled me enough that all they could do was sort of soothe me when I'd start worrying. I couldn't receive more explicit communication until I was off drugs.

A few days later, bulky in my cast, I walked into the hospital with a wad of Canadian currency in my pocket. We'd gotten it by selling an ingot of

Ixmatl gold. I told them I was an American citizen named Charles Barrister, not properly eligible for free Canadian health services, paid my hospital bill, and gave them an erroneous temporary address in Toronto. They scheduled me for outpatient treatment. You never saw hospital people more friendly than they were to this crazy black Yankee who'd come in and paid his bill.

The hospital bill was only the beginning. I backtracked to every damned beekeeper and lumberyard and everyone else I'd ripped off during the defense project, and paid them off, too. Not one asked me any questions when I peeled off those greenbacked bills. Of course, payment was very generous.

Where did the gold come from? I'd explained to Erolanna and the others the principle of war reparations, then had her set Farmond down in the imperial treasury (the guards were *outside* the door, naturally), and he appropriated a large quantity of gold and jewels. Brought back enough to pay not only the hospital and the people I'd ripped off, but the people of Blue River who'd had property stolen or damaged by the enemy, ship owners whose ships had been taken over for our emergency navy, survivor benefits, bonuses to soldiers and sailors, administrative costs for all of this—the whole gamut of legitimate expenses. And healthy awards to the treasuries of Thelmar, Cratlik, and the guardian for their time, trouble, and effort.

And it still left the empire rich.

TWENTY-NINE

An interesting thing about Ixmatl/Earth is that the axial tilt is a lot less than in "my time." I don't know just how much less; I haven't taken the trouble to measure. But roughly it's only about eight or ten degrees now—twelve at most—instead of twenty-three and a half.

The axial poles don't seem to be much different. Gel-Leneth is on the coast of what used to be France at what would have been maybe forty-eight or forty-nine degrees north latitude in the old days. And I noticed that when the calendar indicated the equinox, the sun at midday was about halfway up the meridian. Not much change.

So the winter was pretty mild. The days were somewhat shorter, and it got frosty sometimes at night, but it was pretty mild. There were a couple of inches of snow one morning that melted by noon.

We've made a lot of progress with the time probes over the months, going back and sorting things out for ourselves about the agreement. Quite an experience, believe me. You don't go back and *change* what happened. You go back and *learn* firsthand what happened, and the changes are in today, not in the past. Per the rules of the game.

We gained a lot in individual power and in closeness as a group. We're smarter, happier, and enjoy a lot more confidence. But we're still *us*. I'm still Charley Judge, she's still Erolanna, and so forth. Not that the names are anything more than a convenience, but we're the same individuals, whatever the labels.

Before the leaves had fallen, we'd concluded that we weren't going to wind up the game here with just our little group. The situation is that the points of the agreement weren't written down on something to be found and read. And there were a lot more of them than we'd imagined and an awful lot of booby traps to defuse. Lots of them carried over from older games than Weirro/Earth/Ixmatl. It's a little like an archaeological dig in an old mine field: We find ourselves turning up things layer by layer, very systematically. And there always seems to be another layer underneath, although there is an end to it under there somewhere.

And one good thing about it is that you grow as you go.

And each of us has to find the same things for himself or herself. But the more people doing it, the easier and faster it goes. For example, the first two or three might have a tough time finding a certain thing, but it would be somewhat easier for the ninth and tenth. And the more people that had looked at items A and B and C, the easier it was for the first ones to find D.

Diana's out ahead of course, way ahead, exploring and mapping. She said we needed more instruments and people to use them, and Erolanna and the emeriti got busy making time probes while I went out and got recruits. I went for the brightest people I could find, and then we worked with them until they could work on their own.

By the time the buds were swelling, there were more than a hundred of us, and more kept coming in, especially the young. We built bunks at Amodh Veri; cook had a staff and ran it well (she was probing too, in the evenings), and Cratlik started putting up new people in his castle.

Cratlik! Now there's a guy that changed a ton when he got working with a time probe, though he was still Cratlik—forceful and with a sense of humor, but the meanness and vengefulness shrank and shrank until there was none left.

And like I said, the more people doing it, the easier and faster it goes.

Meanwhile, I've located Shu-Gwelth again. His last defeat really collapsed him, and now he's being a mountain in Bolivia. He erupted last week, destroying a couple of villages with a lava flow and half burying a couple of others with ash. But he's running on automatic now, not really conscious; the mountain might even have blown without him, the way volcanos do.

We monitor him, just in case, but he's really on the bottom. The imprint recorder shows a signature that's little more than a dull spot, and there's almost no halo.

Erolanna's and my signatures? Signatures are *not* a part of the person. Not like fingerprints are part of the body. Back when we were a *lot* more powerful—well before the game of Weirro/Earth/Ixmatl—we created our own signatures. They were like highly individualized hair styles. Aesthetics was strong in those times, and signatures an art form, and the idea was to have no two identical. But then attention went to heavy games, and in time, signatures came to seem unchangeable because we'd lost the power. Way before Earth.

Well, Erolanna and I were together then, too,

and we'd created sort of his/hers signatures. They're alike except for one thing, but the difference didn't show in the imprints because hers had been recorded from behind. They're like mirror images, or optical isomers: We created our signatures to reflect our closeness and yet our difference.

Now the corn is well up. There are more than a hundred and eighty of us here in Cratlik's District, and farmers say the crops look like the best in memory. New batches of recruits are being sent to Gel-Hoveth, where Prince Karn is in charge of training. Karn, who's almost sixteen now, was one of our first recruits and quickest students, and when we found who he'd been, *way* back, it explained a lot.

Things are accelerating, and the top people don't even need probes anymore. They do it without them. The whole thing has the feeling that one of these days it will start to go really fast, like the primacord I used on the Blue River docks. After that, the Weirro/Earth/Ixmatl phase of the broader game will have been handled, and those of us who are ready can go on to the next phase of handling the game of the whole physical universe.

I've ducked out a few times with Diana and Erolanna to look in on other worlds. Some of them are worse than Earth ever was; on some the local game has already been lost. Even long lost. So the new game there will be to handle the old one—dig them out, so to speak. When we're ready.

FRED SABERHAGEN